"Why do you have to be so stubborn... and so beautiful?" he murmured, his lips brushing her forehead.

She pulled away and glared at him. "Beautiful? Stop trying to manipulate me with your phony compliments!"

Rob stared at her, speechless. Then his look of amazement gave way to a tender expression. "Nickie," he said softly, "you've got me all wrong. And you underestimate your powers. But if words won't convince you of my sincerity..."

In one swift movement, he took her in his arms, crushed her to his chest, and brought his lips down on hers. His mouth was like a fiery brand, and against her will desire surged through her body like the pounding of the sea. His practiced lips and hands were urging her to soar with him to the heights of ecstasy.

The passionate kiss ended, but Rob's lips found new pleasures in kissing her cheek, the tip of her nose..."I want you, Nickie," he murmured. "Come home with me..."

Dear Reader:

Two months ago we were delighted to announce the arrival of TO HAVE AND TO HOLD, the thrilling new romance series that takes you into the world of married love. We're pleased to report that letters of praise and enthusiasm are pouring in daily. TO HAVE AND TO HOLD is clearly off to a great start!

TO HAVE AND TO HOLD is the first and only series that portrays the joys and heartaches of marriage. Its unique concept makes it significantly different from the other lines now available to you, and it presents stories that meet the high standards set by SECOND CHANCE AT LOVE. TO HAVE AND TO HOLD offers all the compelling romance, exciting sensuality, and heartwarming entertainment you expect.

We think you'll love TO HAVE AND TO HOLD—and that you'll become the kind of loyal reader who is making SECOND CHANCE AT LOVE an ever-increasing success. Read about love affairs that last a lifetime. Look for three TO HAVE AND TO HOLD romances each and every month, as well as six SECOND CHANCE AT LOVE romances each month. We hope you'll read and enjoy them all. And please keep writing! Your thoughts about our books are very important to us.

Warm Wishes,

Ellen Edwards

Ellen Edwards
SECOND CHANCE AT LOVE
The Berkley Publishing Group
200 Madison Avenue
New York, N.Y. 10016

STARRY EYED
MAUREEN NORRIS

A
SECOND CHANCE AT LOVE
BOOK

STARRY EYED

Copyright © 1983 by Edythe Cudlipp Lachlan

Distributed by The Berkley Publishing Group

First edition published December 1983

First printing

"Second Chance at Love" and the butterfly emblem are trademarks belonging to Jove Publications, Inc.

Printed in the United States of America

Second Chance at Love books are published by
The Berkley Publishing Group
200 Madison Avenue, New York, NY 10016

STARRY EYED

Chapter One

NICKIE MONROE WALKED slowly down Bleecker Street toward Sheridan Square and the restaurant where she was to meet literary agent Louise Patella. Greenwich Village was at its best in early June, she decided. On Bleecker Street the trees were still a pale green, but were rapidly deepening to a verdant summer hue. Petunias and tiny roses bloomed pink and red in tiny garden plots, and the shops and brownstones had a freshly washed look from the previous day's rain. The air was clean, as was the warm breeze that ruffled the sleek Dutch-boy cap of Nickie's black hair.

As she crossed Seventh Avenue, Nickie wondered again what Louise wanted to see her about. Louise was a first-rate agent who handled only best-selling authors— like Gregory Thompson. Nickie grimaced at the thought of Gregory. Unable to stop herself, she paused to look in the windows of the bookstore on the corner of Christopher Street and the square. Sure enough, there was

Gregory's book, *Decade,* with the banner calling it "the novel of the decade, so authentic you 'know' it happened."

Nickie stared at the dust jackets of the books in the window and her own reflection, well aware of the irony of the double image. The slim twenty-nine-year-old woman with the heart-shaped face, high cheekbones, and green eyes had been the invisible hand behind *Decade.* But she had vowed to forget the past, Nickie reminded herself.

Shaking her head in self-reproach, she hurried from the window to the restaurant. Louise, meticulously groomed as always, was waiting for her in a booth. Though Nickie's blue jeans, magenta knit top, and navy blazer were appropriately casual Village attire, she wished she had dressed more formally as she took in Louise's flattering cream silk suit and black-and-cream polka-dot blouse. The agent's gray hair was pulled sharply back in a bun, a style that set off her tanned skin, Mediterranean features, and large dark eyes.

"It's good to see you, Nickie; you're looking well," Louise said warmly. "I'm so glad you were free for lunch."

Nickie smiled. "Thanks for the invitation. All I had planned for the day was a bit of work and maybe an hour or so at 'tar beach' to get some sun."

Louise laughed at the reference to apartment roofs, the favored sunning spots for Manhattan residents who could not afford a summer place at the Hamptons or Fire Island. "How's the novel coming?"

Nickie shrugged. "Good, some days. Others . . . you know how it goes."

"You must let me see it as soon as you have a hundred pages and an outline," Louise urged. "I'm really interested in it."

Nickie looked curiously at the agent. "You mean that, don't you?" she asked thoughtfully.

"Absolutely." Louise's voice was firm. "If you can do half as well on your own..." She flushed under the tan. "Let's have a drink," she said abruptly as the waitress came to the table.

After Nickie had ordered a scotch and water, she considered Louise's unfinished remark, knowing all too well what the agent had meant. Nickie had been fresh out of college when she'd gone to work at an advertising agency as a secretary, the first step toward copywriting, she had hoped. Four years later, her goal attained, she had still been unsatisfied. Copywriting, so challenging at first, had become a monotonous routine. She had started to write articles and submit them for publication, and had even experimented with a novel. Unhappy with the results, she had enrolled in the New School, an institution of higher learning in the Village that offered courses rarely found at more traditional universities, with many evening and Saturday classes.

The teacher of her creative-writing course had been Gregory Thompson, a top editor at a leading publishing house and a writer of amusingly cynical short stories that regularly appeared in chic magazines. Looking back, Nickie wasn't sure whether it had been sexual chemistry or her talent that had drawn Gregory to her. She was now well aware that she had been deeply infatuated with the older man, awed by his success as writer and editor, attracted by his saturnine good looks and dark hair flecked with gray at the temples, and flattered by the attention he paid her. It had been a kind of hero-worship on her part.

After the course was over, they'd continued seeing one another, and their professor-student relationship had evolved into a love affair. When the lease on her uptown apartment was up, it had seemed natural for Nickie to move downtown into the large, inexpensive loft Gregory had in the Village. She was already spending her weekends there, as well as several nights during the week.

Helping Gregory with his novel had followed just as naturally, especially since she could contribute her knowledge of Washington, D.C., the place where she had grown up and the setting for a major part of the novel. When Gregory had suggested she quit her job and devote herself full-time to his book, she had been too lovestruck to consider the pitfalls of such a plan. She had thrown herself into the novel heart and soul, both researching and drafting whole sections of it. She certainly hadn't expected her name to appear on the book with Gregory's, but she *had* expected at least some words of gratitude on the acknowledgments page, and perhaps a dedication. But there had been no acknowledgments page, no dedication; nor had Gregory expressed any personal thanks to her for her aid. Indeed, as soon as bound galleys of the book had been circulated to reviewers and it became clear that Gregory had a best-seller on his hands, he seemed to forget that Nickie had had anything to do with the novel. He didn't ask her to accompany him to any of the glamorous parties to which he was deluged with invitations, and she saw less and less of him at their shared apartment. She was not, therefore, very surprised when he moved out of the loft and out of her life with only a cursory good-bye. By that time, Nickie was thoroughly disillusioned with Gregory, and it was actually a relief to find herself alone.

She had no qualms about staying in the apartment she had shared with Gregory. Rent-controlled lofts were scarce in Manhattan, and living in this one made it possible for her to continue writing. She managed to pay the rent with the income from her articles while she started her own novel. Though initially she had been bitter about the two years she'd devoted to Gregory's book—and to Gregory himself—she now looked upon it as a valuable period of apprenticeship.

While Nickie was pondering her past, Louise had been silent, studying the younger woman as if she knew what was going through her mind. "You got a rotten deal, Nickie. If I had known Gregory was such a heel, I would never have represented him."

Nickie sipped her drink, then smiled. "Sure you would have, Louise. You knew the minute you read the manuscript that *Decade* would be a best-seller, with magazine sales, movie options..."

Louise acknowledged this reminder of her ten percent commission with a sheepish grin. "True, but I would have done it differently." She took a big gulp of her scotch before saying, "Anyway, that's not what I wanted to talk to you about."

Nickie raised her eyebrows. "You don't handle articles, and my novel isn't ready—"

"I know," Louise interrupted. "But in the meantime, you have to live." Her tone was maternal.

"The articles pay pretty well," Nickie said defensively.

"Pretty well? Some do." Louise waved a hand dismissively. "You probably make enough to get by, but only just."

It was Nickie's turn to grin sheepishly. The statement was all too true. More than once she'd had to put her novel aside to take on a typing job.

Her embarrassment must have been obvious, for Louise suddenly changed the subject. "Let's order," she suggested. "How about Coquilles St. Jacques to begin with and then the veal?"

Nickie nodded. She was hungry. At the same time, she was becoming increasingly curious about the reason behind Louise's invitation.

Over the tiny bay scallops in a cream sauce nippy with Emmentaler cheese and laced with white wine, Louise asked, "Have you ever heard of Thomas Robinson Starr?"

Nickie laughed. "Everyone who reads the newspaper or watches television has heard of him!"

"True!" Louise laughed, too. "But what exactly do you know about him?"

Nickie soaked up the last drop of sauce with a piece of French bread, her wide eyes reflective. "Well, he's an industrialist, the head of a conglomerate, a diplomat of sorts. The only thing I haven't heard him called is a politician, although he's supposed to have 'made' several congressmen."

Louise nodded, waiting for the waitress to remove their plates. After ordering a bottle of wine to go with the veal, she prompted, "What else?"

"From the society page and the gossip columns, I gather he's always seen at the best places—and with the best women." Nickie shrugged, completely baffled as to why Louise should question her about Starr. She and the wealthy industrialist scarcely moved in the same orbit.

Louise nodded again. "And?" The waitress had brought their veal and was pouring the wine.

"He's often been accused of being unscrupulous, and a playboy." Nickie shook her head. "The man seems to be a bundle of contradictions." She tasted the veal, which was so tenderly sautéed in a black butter sauce that a knife was almost unnecessary. "Mm—this is delicious," she declared.

Louise was giving all her attention to the food, so Nickie asked no more questions until both plates were clean. Then she said, "I still don't understand why you invited me to lunch, or what Thomas Robinson Starr has to do with anything."

"Would you like coffee and dessert or shall we take a walk through Washington Square?" Louise asked evasively. "We could stop in at one of the cafés, the Figaro perhaps, for cannoli and cappuccino. I have no appointments this afternoon, and I get down to the Village so seldom that I might as well make a day of it."

"Fine," Nickie agreed with a sigh. She had seen enough

of Louise during the last stages of *Decade* to know that
the agent would say what she had to say in her own time.

They were only a few blocks from Sixth Avenue and
Eighth Street. On Eighth Street, one of the main shopping
areas in the Village with its clothing stores, bookshops,
and boutiques, the sidewalk was crowded with pedestrians and an array of sidewalk peddlers selling leather
goods and handmade jewelry. As a result, Nickie and
Louise had little chance to talk as they wove their way
to Washington Square where the arch, newly cleaned of
graffiti, gleamed whitely triumphant in the sunshine.
Around the steps of the fountain in the center of the park,
and even inside the pool area where no water was playing,
a variety of people, both young and old, were taking
advantage of the sunny day.

Louise smiled reminiscently. "It never changes, does
it? I grew up on Mott Street on the Lower East Side
when that area was still Italian, not Chinese, and we used
to come here. No jeans and T-shirts in those days, but
the old people and the winos and the mothers with kids
in strollers were the same."

"And the chess players," Nickie agreed, glancing toward the southwest corner where the stone chess tables
stood in summer heat and winter snow. Every table was
taken, with watchers lined up, silently observing the play.

Louise turned to Nickie, her eyes shrewd. "Let's go
on to Figaro's. I'm beginning to taste that cannoli."

Nickie sighed, letting Louise lead her under the can-
opy of tree branches down the path toward West Fourth
Street. She had never seen Louise so mysterious, and
she was determined to find out the reason for this meeting
with no further delay.

At the Café Figaro, where they sat outside on spindly
chairs at a small metal ice-cream table, Nickie began,
"Louise—"

"I'm sorry. You want to know why I called you."

Louise gave a little laugh. "I guess I'm having trouble getting up the nerve to ask you how you'd feel about working with someone else again."

"No!" Nickie's refusal exploded. "I couldn't—wouldn't—go through that again. You should know better than to ask me, Louise."

"Hey, wait a minute!" The soignée agent held up a hand. "Let me finish. I'm not asking you to collaborate exactly; it would be more like an extended interview."

Nickie shook her head helplessly, her jet-black hair swinging back and forth across her cheeks. "You've lost me."

"It's this way." Louise paused to order cappuccino and the cream-filled, crisp crêpes of cannoli for both of them. Then she leaned eagerly over the table and said, "Thomas Robinson Starr called me last week. It seems he wants an authorized biography written. He's gotten wind of an unauthorized book being done, and he wants to set the record straight. To protect himself, I guess."

"Why doesn't he go to the person who's doing the unauthorized one and—"

"He tried that. They didn't hit it off very well, and Starr has the impression that the writer, Burton Shields, is only interested in slinging mud, regardless of the facts. At any rate, Starr's angry enough to want to commission a rival book."

Nickie bit her underlip as the waiter placed the coffee and pastries in front of them. "Why me?"

"To be honest, Nickie, I suggested a couple of other writers who have already done this sort of thing. Starr met them. One turned him down, and he turned the other down. Personality conflict in both cases, I gather. I told him I had someone else in mind, but I'd have to check first. I couldn't figure out why he called me about this in the first place, but he said he checked around and I had a 'responsible' reputation." She grinned. "Oh, incidentally, the man lives up to his own reputation for

charisma. He could charm the birds out of the trees—
he certainly charmed me."

Nickie gazed out at the passersby. A young woman
of about twenty caught her eye. She had a long black
braid hanging down her back, and was wearing blue jeans
and a sweat shirt. Something about the woman reminded
Nickie of herself at that age. Perhaps it was the eagerness
in her face, as if something important was on the verge
of happening, which was what Gregory had always said
about her.

"It won't be easy," Louise was saying. "I gather he's
willing to be very frank about his business activities, but
his personal life is another matter. You remember, or
maybe you don't, that several years ago he was linked
with an heiress who died suddenly—apparently a suicide. The inquest was kind of hushed up, and there were
rumors implicating Starr in her death. There's probably
nothing to them, but the other writers I sent to Starr told
me he refused to talk about this Joan Weldon at all. In
fact, he became furious when her name was mentioned."

"I remember the lurid headlines in the tabloids," Nickie
said. "It's understandable that Starr would find the subject distasteful. Still, the other book will definitely go
into it, and he'll have to do the same."

"Part of your job will be to convince him of that—
after you've established a good working relationship, of
course." Louise scraped her fork over the plate to get
the last bit of cannoli filling. "Do you want me to set up
an appointment? It won't hurt to talk to him."

"I know. It's just...." Nickie smiled ruefully, memories of the years of working with Gregory washing over
her. "I don't think I want to work with someone else
again, at least not right now."

Louise added a spoonful of sugar to her cappuccino
and stirred it. "Not even if it paid enough to let you live
in style while you pursue your own writing? You haven't
even asked me about the money, Nickie."

Nickie's green eyes widened in surprise. "I guess that proves I'm not a professional yet." She laughed at herself. "Okay, what about the money? Does that mean you have a publisher willing to pay an advance on the idea?"

"No publisher yet—not until I can show what kind of a book it will be. But Starr is willing to pay you twenty-five thousand dollars plus expenses to—"

"No! That's too much. Then I'd be bound to write what he wants, how he wants," protested Nickie. "It would be a vanity book. Poor as I may be, I have some integrity."

"I really think he wants a fair book," Louise contradicted. "His idea is that the writer will live with him, so to speak, travel with him, go to meetings, and then draw his or her own conclusions."

"I'd like to think about it." Nickie pursed her lips. With $25,000, she could pay a lot of rent and still save enough to finish her novel without resorting to any more typing jobs.

"I wish I could give you time, Nickie," Louise said regretfully. "But I can't. In a few days Starr's leaving for an economic development conference in the Caribbean, and he'd like the writer to go with him. So you'd have to see him tomorrow, at his apartment."

Nickie sighed. Her novel was really not going well, despite what she'd told Louise. Maybe some writers could work "starving in a garret," but Nickie could not. Every month it was the same struggle to pay the rent, the same agonized decision to put aside the novel for a while and take on an article—if she could get one—or a typing job. Louise was right: it wouldn't hurt to talk to Starr.

"Well?" the agent asked. "Shall I call him?"

"Yes," Nickie said firmly. "Call him."

Louise got up from the chair, pulling the silk skirt down over her generous hips. After finding the waiter to ask about the telephone, she ordered two more cappuccinos before going inside to make the call.

The coffee arrived along with Louise, who had a big smile on her face. "It's all set. Tomorrow morning at ten. I assume that's okay with you?"

"Yes." Nickie smiled, too, suddenly filled with excitement at the prospect of meeting the intriguing and powerful Thomas Robinson Starr.

2

Chapter Two

BY THE NEXT DAY, however, Nickie had a full-fledged case of the jitters as she pushed through the revolving door of the luxury building on upper Park Avenue where Starr owned a condominium apartment. After leaving Louise the previous afternoon, she had gone home to study her wardrobe. She had tried on several outfits. Some seemed too wintry and others too summery, but she had finally decided on a cream-colored silk and linen knit dress that buttoned up the front to form a turtleneck collar that contrasted modestly with the skirt, which was left open from several inches above the knee. It was a dress, moreover, that she had always felt her best in; the knit emphasized her slender figure, long legs, and small, high breasts. With matching high-heeled bone shoes and shoulder bag, the ensemble was certainly elegant enough for a man with impeccable taste, which Starr was known to have.

Her concern, therefore, was not for how she looked,

but for what she'd say to this formidable man she was about to meet. A night of tossing and turning as she had tried to recall everything she'd ever read or heard about Starr had done little to reassure her. But as she stepped onto the elevator after the man behind the desk had called to confirm her appointment, she suddenly smiled. It was silly to be worried about the outcome, since she wasn't even sure that she wanted the job.

Pressing the buzzer beside the heavy paneled door to Starr's penthouse apartment, Nickie steeled herself for the moment when she would meet her potential employer. Before she had time to do much more than smooth her bangs, the door was opened by a middle-aged, heavy-set man in the green baize vest, white shirt, and dark trousers of a movie houseman. Nickie gave her name and the houseman nodded, leading her to a terrace overlooking the city with the East River sparkling in the sunlit distance. In the center of the terrace, a glass-topped, wrought-iron table was set for breakfast for two. Nickie wondered if she should sit down at one of the two matching chairs, but that seemed too casual so she wandered to the edge of the terrace and stood there gazing at the view.

"Good morning, Ms. Monroe."

Nickie turned at the sound of a deep, resonant voice that made her stomach do an unaccustomed flip-flop. And when she saw the speaker, the flip-flop was followed by a double somersault. Newspaper photographs had shown Thomas Robinson Starr to be a handsome man— tall and broad-shouldered, with the physique of an athlete and the chiseled features of a matinee idol. But no photograph could capture the sensual gleam in the cobalt-blue eyes that looked out from his deeply tanned face, or the dazzling intimacy of the smile he bestowed on her like a caress.

Nickie suddenly remembered the Arthurian legends that had so fascinated her in childhood and realized with

a shock that the man before her corresponded almost
exactly to her image of Sir Lancelot. There was even the
same air of youthful idealism she had associated with
the romantic knight, making Starr seem much younger
than his thirty-eight years. The boyish image was reinforced by the impetuous way he ran one long-fingered
hand through the short waves of his chestnut hair. Where
were the graying temples she had imagined, and where
was the three-piece Savile Row suit she had expected
him to be wearing? Here she had dressed to the nines to
equal Starr in elegance, and he had come to greet her in
a vivid blue polo shirt that matched his eyes and an
immaculate pair of white denim pants that hugged his
slim hips and long legs like a second skin. Yet instead
of making her feel overdressed, the scrutiny of those
clear, piercing eyes made Nickie feel she had been trans-
formed into a ravishing beauty as if by a magic wand.
Not that she wasn't accustomed to male admiration, but
Nickie knew herself to be more gamin than siren. "My
little cutie," Gregory used to call her affectionately. Now
why did the phrase come to her mind voiced in Starr's
sexy baritone rather than Gregory's reedy tenor? She
mustn't allow herself to get any romantic ideas about
Thomas Robinson Starr. He might be Lancelot, but she
was no Guinevere, and as for that look . . . well, the man
was a womanizer; he probably looked at every attractive
female that way.

"Mr. Starr?" With an uncharacteristically formal nod,
Nickie at last managed to acknowledge him.

"That's right." He strode toward her and took her right
hand in his, but not for the handshake Nickie expected.
Rather, his warm fingers merely clasped hers, and then,
like the gallant knight he evoked for her, he led her to
the table and held out one of the wrought-iron chairs.
"Won't you sit down?" he asked, his eyes continuing to
appraise her from head to toe as if he couldn't look
away—and didn't want to. And did she only imagine

that he held her hand longer than necessary before she seated herself in the chair?

"Thank you." She watched as he sat down across from her, again ruffling his hair with the strangely endearing gesture. Even more strangely, she felt an overpowering urge to ruffle it for him. Stifling the impulse, she told herself that it was just that Starr was so different from her image of the shrewd, tough manipulator who had bankrolled a modest inheritance into a fortune by taking over a string of small companies and making them profitable. At least now she understood why women found him so attractive. Despite a stern warning to herself that *she* mustn't be attracted to him, Nickie felt her resistance to doing the biography fading as she waited, pulses racing, for him to speak.

"Breakfast should arrive shortly," he said, flashing her a disarming smile. At that very moment the houseman appeared bearing a large silver tray. "I hope you like strawberries," Starr went on, as the houseman set down the tray, the centerpiece of which was a large crystal bowl of perfectly formed, lusciously ripe strawberries. There was also a silver coffeepot placed over an alcohol burner, a basket of brioches and croissants wrapped in a damask napkin, a crock of sweet butter, small crystal bowls of honey and marmalade, and a silver sugar bowl and matching creamer.

"My favorite fruit," Nickie admitted, smiling back at him, "but these look almost too good to eat."

Before she knew it, one of the sweet red berries was on her tongue, and with it the warm, slightly salty taste of Starr's finger, which, she realized in astonishment, was withdrawing from her mouth—with considerably less haste than it had arrived.

Starr met her startled gaze with a playful wink. "Sorry," he said, his tone belying his words. "I just didn't want you to be bashful about digging in."

His action had created a cocoon of intimacy around

them that Nickie felt she must immediately dissolve. But suspecting that her own initial formality had only goaded Starr into taking the liberty, she decided to break the spell with a bit of humor. After taking time to chew and swallow the berry, she said lightly, "I stand corrected. These strawberries are too good *not* to eat," and helped herself to another.

"So are the croissants," he said, putting one of the flaky crescent rolls on a plate for her. "And Burns brews a superb pot of coffee," he continued, pouring her a cup of the dark brew. Nickie suddenly had a suspicion that she was being manipulated; his ostensible hospitality had the effect of reducing her to utter passivity while he took control of the interview. But before she could seize the initiative, he had poured cream into her coffee—really, the man's hands moved like lightning—and was about to add sugar as well when she finally found her voice.

"Just the cream, thanks," she said firmly. "I don't care for sweetened coffee."

"No? I do." One hand held the sugar tongs in midair, while he poured some coffee for himself with the other and then added the sugar. "I enjoy all the sweet things of life," he confided, gazing at her in a way that suggested he considered *her* one of life's "sweet things."

Realizing it was a come-on—more playful than Gregory's approach, but none the less blatant for that—Nickie wondered why she didn't feel angry. Worse, why did she feel as if she were melting beneath his gaze faster than the sugar had melted in his coffee?

"I hope sharing all your tastes isn't a prerequisite to writing your biography?" she inquired, hoping to steer the conversation toward the business that had brought her here.

But Starr was apparently in no hurry to get down to brass tacks—or perhaps he merely wanted to show her who was boss. "Not a prerequisite," he drawled, "but I do think our mutual predilection for strawberries is a hopeful omen." As he spoke, he reached for one of the juicy berries, and Nickie's hand instinctively went to her mouth as if to ward him off. But with an amused glint in his eye, he popped the berry into his own mouth and savored it with a maddening air of nonchalance.

Nickie pretended to cough into her hand. "Are you a believer in omens, then, Mr. Starr?" she chaffed him. She felt a need to show that she could not only take his teasing but could dish out some of her own.

"When it suits me to be," he answered genially, sipping his coffee as he watched her butter a croissant. "You have such graceful fingers, Ms. Monroe. Tell me, do you play the piano?"

Nickie was thrown off guard. "Actually, I do," she answered. "That is, I used to, but since I don't have an instrument in my apartment..." Her voice trailed off as she wondered how *she* had become the subject of their conversation.

"Oh, but I have one here," he said, smiling. "I play a little myself, so perhaps we could try a duet sometime."

The invitation was so fraught with innuendo that Nickie decided to abandon subtlety and simply take charge of the interview. "Mr. Starr, I thought we were here to discuss working together, rather than playing together. And if that's the case, well, surely you're a very busy man..."

She was unexpectedly disappointed when his engaging smile abruptly disappeared and he took on a businesslike demeanor. "You're quite right, Ms. Monroe; this is a business appointment. Now, can you tell me why you're interested in writing this book?"

She had anticipated the question and gave an honest answer. "Well, I *am* a writer, and you've offered very favorable terms, not to mention the boost to my career an opportunity like this might provide."

"Good. I didn't think you'd start spouting any malarkey about your long, intense interest in me, the way that first writer of Louise's did, but I wanted to be sure. I'm a straightforward man, Ms. Monroe, and I like the people who work for me to be equally direct."

Nickie nodded. Much to her relief, he seemed unaware that she *did* have an intense interest in him—one that had been sparked by nothing loftier than sheer animal magnetism.

"Now, Louise has told me all about your advertising experience, your previous publications—in short, all about Nickie Monroe the writer. Suppose you tell me about Nickie Monroe the person."

The request, which was issued more as a command, startled her. "What would you like to know?" she asked, raising her coffee cup to her lips to play for time.

"As much as you'll tell me. After all, I'll be telling you all of *my* secrets," he said ironically, "so it's only fair that I learn a few of yours."

She wondered if this was an indication that he intended the biography to give his version of the Joan Weldon affair after all, but decided this wasn't the moment to pursue the matter. Instead, she answered lightly, "I don't quite follow your logic. After all, you wish to be the subject of a biography; I don't. I'll be happy to discuss my professional credentials with you, of course, and I've brought along some copies of interviews I've written up for you to look at, but I don't see where my personal life has any relevance at all."

He quirked an eyebrow at her. "Really, Ms. Monroe, I'm not asking for any intimate confessions. But I do like to know something about the people I work with. Surely you can tell me where you come from, for instance, and perhaps something about your family and your hobbies. Would that constitute an invasion of your privacy?" he asked sarcastically.

She supposed her reluctance to talk about herself stemmed from embarrassment, but his sarcasm stung, and she answered perversely, "Well, you already know one of my hobbies—piano playing."

"Are you being coy, Ms. Monroe—or just snippy?"

"Just snippy," she responded pertly, wondering at herself. Yet somehow she feared that even the most innocuous personal revelations would suddenly bring back the feeling of intimacy that had enveloped them earlier.

Starr abruptly began to laugh heartily, and it was some time before his merriment ceased. "I even like your stubborn streak—it's a match for my own. But"—he paused —"if you want the job, you'll have to yield gracefully on this one."

She was surprised at just how much she did want the job now, and she knew that for all his affability he was speaking seriously. With equal seriousness, she said, "All right then, to take your questions in order: I come from Rockville, Maryland—that's just outside Washington—and I lived there till I moved to New York seven years ago. My parents still live in Rockville—my father's a piano tuner and my mother's a secretary—but my brothers and sisters have all moved, too."

When he opened his mouth to speak, she thought he was going to tell her to never mind about the brothers and sisters, but instead he asked, "You come from a large family then?" She thought he sounded wistful.

"Three brothers and two sisters," she affirmed.

"Are you close to any of them?"

Nickie shrugged. "It's somewhat hard to stay close when we're all scattered over different parts of the country, but we do have rather jolly holiday gatherings and that kind of thing. I enjoy catching up with everyone when we get together. To be truthful, though, as a kid I resented having so many siblings. I'm one of the middle children, and I always had to share a room with one or two sisters. And with six of us, there was just so much *noise*. I used to retreat to the backyard and climb up a tree with a book so I could read in peace for a change. I was the family bookworm," she explained.

"And the family tomboy." He grinned. "You know, I can picture you scrambling up that tree with your book. You still have something of a hoyden look about you."

Nickie frowned. Why should she care if he still saw traces of the tomboy she had been? Nevertheless, the remark deflated her.

"What kinds of books did you read?" Starr continued.

"Oh, anything I could get my hands on," she said blithely, not wanting to admit her marked preference for romances. That might lead into inquiries about her love life, past and present, and she wasn't about to discuss that subject with Starr, job or no job.

But she needn't have worried. He asked her a few more questions—about her childhood, her four years at American University, and her decision to move to New York. He answered the last question himself, accurately: "But then where else would an aspiring copywriter go?" Finally, he sat back in his chair and said, "All right, now, I'd like to look at those writing samples you mentioned."

Nickie took the clippings from her purse and handed them across the table. Their hands touched briefly during the transfer, and she felt an involuntary thrill course through her body. Lord, she scolded herself, if an accidental meeting of fingers could make her feel as if a Christmas tree had been lit up inside her, what would a kiss from this magnetic man do to her? Not that she planned to find out, she hastily amended.

As Starr began to read the first clipping, Nickie poured herself another cup of coffee. When he failed to comment after finishing the article and going on to another one, she began to feel apprehensive—maybe he didn't like her approach to the interviews, or didn't care for her writing style. But when he had read all three clippings, the handsome industrialist gave her another of his bone-melting smiles and said abruptly, "I take it you're free to start immediately?"

Nickie was caught off balance. "You mean you want me to do the biography?"

His diffident shrug dampened her elation. "Frankly, I don't want anyone to do the biography. I mean, I don't want one done at all. But since this Shields character is going ahead with his lurid exposé whether I like it or not . . . well, I have to tell my own story."

Nickie's apprehension returned. "Look, Mr. Starr, I wouldn't feel comfortable with a first-person narrative, or even an as-told-to—"

"No, no," he interrupted. "I was merely using a figure of speech. You do the writing. It's to be a straightforward biography—only I have to approve it for publication, you understand. I like the way you handled these interviews," he said, gesturing at the pile of clippings by his coffee cup, "but a biography, of course, is more than just an extended interview."

"Of course," said Nickie, relieved that *he* understood that. Still, she wondered if his open lack of enthusiasm for the project would make it difficult—or even impossible—for her to do a really comprehensive book.

Starr sighed and motioned toward the clippings again. "Look," he said, "these tell me you have a lively style, a certain respect for other people—that is, you're no mud-slinger like Shields—but I'd already gathered that from my conversation with Louise. The real question is whether you'll write about me in a way I find acceptable, and I can't truly gauge that until you've written something and I've read it. Now, I want you to get to know me: travel with me, live with me . . ." His voice trailed off and his square face flushed under the tan as he realized the suggestive implication of his words.

Nickie found herself laughing at his embarrassment despite herself, as she took another bite of croissant. "I thought you didn't want an exposé," she teased.

He laughed, too, obviously relieved by her reaction. "At least you have a sense of humor," he commented appreciatively. "My idea is for you to accompany me on business trips, see how I operate, stay here when I'm in the city and have time to fill you in on my background."

Nickie studied him. Staying at his penthouse with him was out of the question after Gregory. She was more concerned at the moment, however, with finding out how far he would let her go in writing the biography. "Does that mean I can interview or talk to anyone I think could help to . . . balance your version of yourself?" Without that freedom, she knew she would have to refuse the job, regardless of the way Starr was arousing her curiosity— and other, more dangerous, emotions.

The tycoon hesitated. "Some people aren't exactly unprejudiced where I'm concerned. A few of them would say anything . . ."

Nickie wondered if, after all, there was some foundation for the sinister rumors circulating about this man. Were his business practices really unscrupulous, and had he somehow been responsible for Joan Weldon's death? "I don't listen to gossip," she said guardedly. "I would never use anything that was not in the record or couldn't be proved. But you don't live or work in a vacuum. A biography is facts: you, other people, and—"

"We're going around in circles, aren't we?" Starr took a brioche and buttered it slowly. "I have a suggestion," he said finally. "Tell me what you think of it."

"Very well." Nickie leaned forward in her chair and met his gaze.

His brilliant eyes were mesmerizing. "As you probably know, I've already spoken to two other writers. Both were men, I might add. We couldn't get together for a variety of reasons. I'm not sure that you and I can, but I don't have time to go on talking to writers—not with Burton Shields breathing down my neck and doing his best to dig up dirt on me." He paused, as if to assess her reaction to these remarks.

Nickie's eyes remained locked with his, the contact

sending a warm flow of longing through her. Not trusting her voice, she nodded. According to Louise, Shields was the kind of writer who would stop at nothing short of libel if it would sell more books.

The faint smile on Starr's mobile mouth turned into a wide one. "I suggest," he said softly, "that you come to the meeting in Curaçao with me. It's an economic and development conference of hemisphere businessmen, with a few government officials attending. You can watch what goes on, and then we can talk." His eyes twinkled as if in anticipation of her and her company.

Nickie's pulses raced wildly at the invitation in that seductive smile. She had known that traveling with Starr would be part of the job, but the obvious sensual attraction between them made the setup seem a good deal more intimate than Louise had implied. "I could do that," she said slowly, her mind in a turmoil.

"I haven't finished," he cautioned, as her pulses slowed in expectation of a condition she might not want to meet. "Naturally, I'll pay your expenses and a fee for your time. In return, I want you to write something up to give me an idea of how you'd approach the book. In other words, we'd both be on trial."

The tone of his voice and the light in his eyes were almost cajoling, and Nickie was more curious than ever to find out what Thomas Robinson Starr was really like. The trip would be a test in more ways than one, and she would have to be careful to avoid getting involved in any relationship that could endanger their professional collaboration.

Still, if she were alert to the pitfalls, she might enjoy being constantly under the spell of the charismatic industrialist. Nickie was suddenly conscious of how utterly lacking in excitement her life had been lately. She quickly brushed aside the thought, and tried to concentrate on the biography instead. She had no way of knowing whether she would find this type of writing congenial. The only way to find out would be by trying. The challenge exhilarated her.

"Well, what do you say?" Starr reached across the table to take her hand.

A current of desire seemed to flow from his fingers to hers. "Yes," she answered slowly. Whatever happened, she wanted to explore the enigma of Thomas Robinson Starr, the cold-hearted tycoon and the obviously warm-blooded man.

"Good." He stood up. "My car will pick you up Monday at nine in the morning."

Nickie realized she was being dismissed. His mercurial mood changes confused her. His suddenly aloof manner was a blow to her ego, while the longings stirred in her by his warm smiles and looks had been definitely threatening. As he saw her to the door of the penthouse, she made up her mind that when she was with him in the future, she would concentrate on the biography.

As he held the door for her, Nickie smiled. "I'll see you on Monday, then."

He nodded, with a caress of his blue eyes that sent an electric current charging once more through every fiber of her being. "I'm looking forward to it." He paused, taking her hand and holding it. "You'll need some formal attire—and don't forget your bathing suit . . . Nickie."

Nickie could feel the blood rushing to her face at his use of her first name and his lingering touch. She hastily withdrew her hand. "I'll remember," she said quickly, hurrying to the elevator. She hoped that in time he would cease to have such an unnerving effect on her senses, but if he didn't . . . well, like Scarlett O'Hara, she would just have to think of that tomorrow.

Chapter Three

By eight-thirty Monday morning, Nickie was packed and waiting for the car to pick her up. As she put on the pink cotton summer suit with the matching pink-and-white checked blouse that she had decided would be appropriate for the plane, she glanced around the loft.

Her apartment was on the fifth floor of a former industrial building on the westernmost edge of Greenwich Village, with a good view of the Hudson River. Although the two bedrooms that Gregory had had built were small, the main room was spacious and airy, with high ceilings and a skylight. In front of the windows was a working area with a large desk, several file cabinets, overflowing bookcases, and a metal stand with an electric typewriter. On the opposite wall was the kitchen, separated from the living area by a long, coffee-shop-style counter with several stools. In the center of the room were two large couches, both of which had seen better days, with faded cretonne slipcovers and sagging upholstery. A couple of wingback chairs, only slightly more respectable, and what Gregory had euphemistically called a "home entertainment center," with a stereo and television set, completed the furnishings. The floor was bare except for an old Persian carpet and a few assorted scatter rugs.

Nickie made a face at the room, thinking how wonderful it would be to get away from it for a while, After months of living and working here, it was beginning to seem like a prison at times. The only saving grace was the extension of the roof beyond the wall with the windows. She had fixed it up as well as she could with an old hibachi and a couple of folding chairs she had found on the street. When work and the walls pressed in on her, she would escape to this "tar beach," to lie in the sun and dream that she was somewhere exotic—like Curaçao, where she actually would be in a matter of hours, she thought with a smile.

The ringing of the buzzer connecting the apartment with the lobby downstairs broke into her thoughts. Nickie picked up her suitcase and hurried to the hall. Locking the door behind her, she felt her heart beat faster. She pushed the button for the elevator and impatiently tapped her foot as she heard the old cage creak and groan its way to her floor. Starr did not seem like a man who appreciated being kept waiting.

To her relief, however, the only person in the lobby was Starr's houseman, Burns, who apparently doubled as chauffeur. He smiled and took her suitcase, putting it in the trunk of the stretch Lincoln Continental limousine with smoked-glass windows.

"Good morning, Miss Monroe," he said politely with a slight British accent. "Mr. Starr had to make a few long-distance calls. Rather than make you wait, he sent me to pick you up."

"That was very considerate of him," murmured Nickie, feeling a bit overwhelmed. The man held the door open for her as she got into the luxurious, roomy, air-conditioned limousine.

By the time the car had reached Starr's building and the houseman had left her to get his employer's luggage and to find out if Starr was ready to leave, Nickie's earlier exhilaration had turned to apprehension. Her trepidation was not relieved by Starr's arrival. In his tailored gray slacks, blue blazer over a white polo shirt, and Italian loafers, he looked every inch the millionaire tycoon. But when he smiled at her, she felt reassured. Well, perhaps reassured wasn't exactly the word she ...

"We'll be leaving from Teterboro Airport," he told her in his resonant baritone. "That's in New Jersey, not far from Newark. It's a small airport used exclusively by charters and private aircraft."

"How long a flight is it?" she asked. Although she knew that Curaçao was in the Netherlands Antilles, a small string of islands off the Venezuelan coast, she was hazy about the distance.

"About four or five hours in the jet, nonstop." Starr's eyes were looking at her approvingly, moving from the black cap of her hair to her slim, feminine body and long, slender legs. "During the flight I have to do some reading to prepare for the conference, so we won't be able to talk much."

Nickie frowned, trying to ignore the admiration on his face as his gaze lingered on her legs. "I thought the point of my going with you was that we *would* be able to talk, Mr. Starr," she reminded him.

"We'll have plenty of time for that later," he replied. "This flight is my only chance to brief for the conference. By the way, stop calling me Mr. Starr. My friends call me Rob."

Nickie nodded, her heart beating faster at the thought of being on a first-name basis with the dashing tycoon. Yet he was obviously not eager to work on the biography or talk about himself. If he persisted in putting her off, she would have no alternative but to talk to the other members of the conference and rely on their accounts to write the sample chapters Starr himself had requested.

Lost in her thoughts, she didn't notice that they had driven through the Holland Tunnel and were approaching Teterboro until the limousine drew to a halt by an office in the front of a large hangar. Burns opened her door, while Starr got out on the other side. He told her to wait and went into the office, returning shortly with three men in dark blue trousers and white shirts. The two with the gold wings on their left-hand pockets had to be the pilot and copilot, Nickie assumed, while the third was probably a steward.

She speculated for a moment about the private jet Starr had mentioned. It couldn't be the six-passenger Lear jet she had noticed standing in front of the hangar, but she was still startled to see the four men walk toward a Gulfstream 2 waiting at the end of the runway, with stairs rolled up to the door. Burns started toward it, carrying the luggage and Starr's briefcase, and she followed.

After boarding the aircraft, Nickie glanced around, not really surprised at the luxurious appointments, considering the penthouse and limousine. A galley separated the cockpit and a comfortable lounge area with tables high and large enough to serve as desks, flanked by cozy armchairs. Behind the lounge, on each side of what would have been the aisle in a regular aircraft, were two groupings of small armchairs around cocktail tables. And at the rear was a curtain leading to what were probably sleeping cabins.

Nickie barely had time to seat herself in a chair in the lounge across from Starr and the steward before the plane began rumbling down the runway. As soon as they were airborne and at cruising altitude, the steward disappeared into the galley. Starr, with a smile that painted rainbows inside Nickie's heart, picked up his briefcase.

"Jim will have coffee and rolls in a minute, Nickie. In the meantime"—he handed her a sheaf of papers— "you might want to take a look at these. They're the agenda for the conference and the guest list, plus brief bios of the participants."

"Thanks," she said with an answering smile as she took the papers. This time she was sure that Starr's hand rested on hers a moment longer than necessary before he relinquished the papers and turned his attention to some other documents.

Nickie leafed through the material, looking for the biographies. Thomas Robinson Starr's contained nothing that Louise had not told her, omitting, of course, any mention of his love life.

The steward returned with coffee in a thermos jug, warm brioches, honey, and sweet butter, along with two china cups and saucers, then disappeared again. Nickie helped herself to coffee and nibbled on a buttery brioche, pretending to study the papers while she pondered what she had already learned about Starr. On Saturday, she had gone to the library to read whatever she could find about him, starting with the *Who's Who* entry that gave the bare facts. From the business magazines and news weeklies, she had learned that his mother had died just after his birth. He had attended Exeter, an exclusive school in New England, and had dropped out of Princeton University in his senior year when his father died, leaving him a small tool-and-die business. Within five years, he had bought out his major competitor after a price war between the two that had ended with the competitor being forced to sell or go bankrupt. Starr's decision to modernize operations had led to his buying a computer company. From that beginning, he had branched out into mining and drilling rights and leases. If the tool-and-die company was the basis of his business empire, the rights and leases were the basis of his wealth. An avocation, if you could call it that, was politics, dating from his days as a political-science major at Princeton, and he often backed senators and congressmen whose views he favored, regardless of party. As a result, he had served more than once on diplomatic trade missions.

The private Thomas Robinson Starr was more elusive. He had never been married, preferring to play the field with a seemingly endless string of heiresses and actresses, a combination that Nickie found amusing. The one thing all the women had in common was their beauty. The only hint of a genuine romance had been with Joan Weldon, the heiress Louise had mentioned. For close to a year his name had been linked with hers. On the night of her death he had escorted her to the opening of a Broadway play. Rob had testified at the closed inquest her parents managed to arrange, but to the reporters gathered outside he would only say, "No comment." That had been three years ago. Since then, Starr had played the field, with no indications of another serious love affair.

"Those papers must be more engrossing than I thought." Rob's voice was amused.

Nickie looked up with a start to see his eyes on her with the intent expression she found so disturbing. She noticed that he had put aside his work. Trying to smile, she said, "I wish I knew more about economics, trade barriers, and tariffs, the kind of thing you'll be talking about in Curaçao."

Rob leaned back, a smile lifting the corners of his expressive mouth. "I don't expect you to write a treatise, Nickie, only a sample chapter or two that will show me how you intend to handle the book."

"Then talk to me," Nickie urged, leaning forward, her green eyes large and bright in her heart-shaped face. "I can't write about you until I know you."

"We'll have plenty of time for that later," he said again. "First, I want you to attend the conference." He linked his hands behind his neck, totally at ease and in control of himself.

"But we have some time now," Nickie protested. "You've finished your reading and—"

"And I need to unwind a bit," he interrupted. "You know, I usually spend the last hour or so of these flights just humming or singing old folksongs to myself. But since you're here, why don't we sing together?"

"You want me to sing folksongs with you?" Nickie asked incredulously.

"Why not? It passes the time, it's relaxing, and there was some mention of us doing a musical duet the other day."

"A piano duet, and you're the one who mentioned it," she reminded him. "I didn't agree."

For answer, he burst into the opening bars of "Molly Malone." The Irish ballad was a favorite of Nickie's, and by the time Starr reached the refrain she couldn't resist joining in. As they went on to "Loch Lomond" and "Oh! Susanna," Starr let her carry the melody line in her light soprano while his rich baritone improvised a harmony.

As they sang ballad after ballad, Nickie had to admit that she was enjoying herself, and was also enjoying Starr's enjoyment as he sang out with gusto, his face taking on the boyish cast she found so appealing.

After a boisterous rendition of "She'll be Comin' Round the Mountain," Starr said suddenly, "Time for a change of mood." It was soon clear what mood he had in mind, as he began to croon "Drink to Me Only With Thine Eyes" in a seductive manner, gazing soulfully at Nickie as he sang, and lingering on the words *kiss* and *thine*.

Despite her resolve to view Starr merely as her employer and the subject of her book, Nickie felt a warm, romantic glow as he serenaded her. But when the song was over, she said firmly, "I'm getting a bit hoarse. That will have to be all for now."

"What a pity," Starr drawled, "when we make such beautiful music together." He reached for her hand and brought it to his lips.

His mouth was warm and moist as he kissed the back of her hand, and Nickie felt a shiver of pleasure travel up her arm. "A tribute to your lovely voice," Starr explained as he slowly released her hand. "I look forward to finding out all your other lovely qualities," he added suggestively.

"I'm the one who's supposed to be finding out about your qualities," she reminded him tartly, thinking it safer to ignore his compliment and its implications.

He grinned. "Oh, you will. You will."

"I mean for the book," she said, wondering how she was going to maintain her objectivity when Rob's every look and gesture communicated an intimacy that belied their professional relationship.

"Only for the book? You know, Nickie, ours is a somewhat unusual working relationship. We're going to get to know each other pretty well, and I don't see why we shouldn't be . . . friends."

"I don't think it would be wise for us to . . ." She flushed as his eyes seemed to caress her body. "To be too friendly."

Rob laughed, a rumble of pleasure that seemed to start in his deep chest. "I have one enemy in Burton Shields. I don't want another one, Nickie. Especially not my *authorized* biographer."

"That isn't what I meant!" Blood rushed to her face.

The smile lingered on Rob's lips. "Try it my way," he urged, intimacy again shading every word.

Nickie bit her lip. The blush had receded, but her heart was beating a rapid tattoo, despite her realization that he was not treating the book seriously enough. He seemed to expect the biography to roll effortlessly from his lips through her to the typewriter. Her spine stiffened resolutely in protest. "I thought," she said in a firm, soft voice, "that you hired me because I'm a professional writer, to write *my* way..."

The warm blue eyes suddenly turned icy in a silence almost ominous with tension. He frowned and then said sharply, as the plane's wheels were lowered with a thump, "We're almost there. You'd better fasten your seat belt."

Nickie did as she was told. Tossing her head stubbornly, she looked out the window and saw low, craggy hills covered with straggly brush falling off to a flat sandy strip along the shore. To the right of the long runway and the cluster of low airport buildings was the deep, shimmering blue of the Caribbean stretching into the distance to meet the sky on the horizon.

The plane landed, taxiing past the terminal to an apron on which stood several private planes, all much smaller than Starr's jet. Almost immediately a staircase was rolled to the door, which the steward opened to let in a blast of hot air. Waiting below was an official who waved Starr and his party through immigration and customs, escorting them to a car and driver. Within moments, their luggage was in the trunk, and the car was speeding along a two-lane road toward the main town of Willemstad on the other side of the island. They were staying at the Hilton, where the conference was to be held, a few miles outside Willemstad. Nickie got only a glimpse of the capital of the Antilles from a high bridge over the deep natural channel that bisected the town as it led from the Caribbean to a large harbor.

The hotel was almost a small town itself, set on beautifully landscaped grounds. Hibiscus and other tropical bushes and flowers bloomed in a riot of color under the scanty shade of graceful palm trees. At the entrance, Nickie and Rob were met by the hotel manager. He had obviously been waiting for them, and he whisked them ceremoniously to an enormous suite that overlooked the pool, a steep hill of a beach on a tiny lagoon, and the fantastically blue ocean.

Nickie looked around. Spectacular as the view was, the suite was plainly furnished in typically American hotel style, with teal blue and orange predominating. To her, the main attraction was the small terrace, from which a cool trade wind blew into the room. When she turned, Rob was watching her, his face lit up by a questioning smile as he waited for her comment.

"It's very nice," Nickie told him formally. She eyed him suspiciously as the manager disappeared. "What about my room?" She had no intention of "living with him" as he had suggested at their first meeting.

"Here . . ."

"Here?" Nickie could feel fury blazing in her eyes. "I came to Curaçao to work, Mr. Starr," she fumed, "not to be your—"

"Wait a minute!" Rob crossed the room in a couple of strides and put his hands on her shoulders. "Don't jump to conclusions. I know why you're here, why I asked you to come." He stared at her, the wall of tension between them as charged as an electric fence. The warmth in his eyes turned to surprise, and he dropped his hands as if he had burned them.

Nickie felt her anger change subtly to a painful longing. Her shoulders tingled from his touch, and the closeness of his powerful body sent a tremor of excitement down her spine. Her pounding heart seemed to stop beating for a moment before pounding more erratically as a quivering flame of desire ignited within her. Starr's lips parted slightly and he stepped back, a dazed expression in his eyes.

"Didn't I tell you to call me Rob?" he asked, running a hand through his chestnut hair. He seemed to be trying to regain his composure of a few minutes earlier, as he nodded toward some bottles standing on a sideboard with an ice bucket and a bowl of fruit. "How about a drink?"

"First, where—" Nickie began, recalling how Gregory had invited her to the loft the first time to talk to her about his novel, except that the novel had been forgotten until the next morning.

Rob ignored her. "Is scotch and soda all right?" He was busy opening the bottle and pouring liquor into two glasses. He added ice and soda and handed her one before taking a big sip of his.

"Sit down, Nickie." He nodded toward a chair and settled himself on a matching sofa, keeping a low cocktail table between them. When she obeyed, not knowing what else to do, he said, "Your room is across the hall, here in the hotel. I didn't mean it the way it sounded."

Nickie studied him, her legs still shaking. "I see," she said slowly. "Why didn't you say that in the beginning?"

"It never occurred to me that you would think I meant *here!*" He sounded chagrined, and his smile was tinged with embarrassment. "Believe it or not, that's the truth." He set his glass down, leaning forward to reach across the table and take her hand.

Once more, a tongue of flame surged through Nickie. She withdrew her hand hastily. "Very well," she said, standing up. "I think I'll have a look at my room now," she told him, hoping her voice sounded light. Rob raised an eyebrow quizzically, and Nickie felt her face burn as she turned on her heel and marched across the hall.

Placing the key in the door, she thought how silly she was being. Why would a man like Thomas Robinson Starr want to seduce her, when wealthy socialites and glamorous movie stars were his for the asking? His charming manner could be a kind of game for him, a frivolous exercise of his romantic powers. Well, he would be exercising them in vain, Nickie told herself. Gregory had used and discarded her, and she wasn't going to suffer a second humiliation at the hands of Rob Starr.

Chapter Four

As Nickie showered and dressed for the cocktail party that marked the opening of the conference, she kept telling herself that she was only an employee to Starr. That thought was more difficult to keep in mind as the evening wore on, even though Rob kept introducing her as a writer covering the conference for him. For one thing, from the moment he picked her up at her room, he treated her with all the deference and charm for which he was noted in the newspaper columns. For another, as she stood next to him in the cocktail lounge, the closeness of his athletic, virile body sent a warm glow through her, and an accidental brush of his hand made her knees go weak with yearning. His reluctance to leave her side only increased the warmth to a fever pitch, as she forced herself to pay attention to the introductions and the conversation that followed.

Nevertheless, the cocktail party gave Nickie the beginning of an insight into the complex tycoon. With the

diplomats, he was urbane, keeping to generalities as the
Americans tried to enlist him on the side of self-help,
while their counterparts from the Caribbean and Central
and South America less than subtly tried to get him to
take a position favoring loans to their governments. With
the businessmen, he fell back on technical talk of oil
prices and labor-intensive industry to produce employ-
ment as opposed to mechanization that replaced workers.
Several of the men were accompanied by their wives,
and to them he was all dazzling charm. As a result, Nickie
was able to reassure herself that his flirtatious manner
with her meant nothing. To her surprise, however, the
reassurance did not subdue the excitement she felt when-
ever his eyes captured hers or his hand lightly touched
her back as he steered her from one group to another.

Even so, Nickie managed to glean some information
as they moved about the room. She made a mental note
of names, gradually becoming aware that not everyone
was glad to see Rob. She resolved to speak to a few of
those who seemed less than friendly, in particular a South
American oilman and a California computer executive
named Nils Claussen. Yes, she must get their views on
Thomas Robinson Starr.

When it came time for dinner, Nickie was left to her
own devices. A place had been reserved for Rob on the
dais, while she was seated at a large table in the rear of
the ballroom. Because of the speeches, she had little
chance to talk to any of her dinner companions.

After coffee, she rose to her feet, not sure what to do
next. As she saw Rob striding purposefully toward her,
her heart began to pound irrationally. Sudden joy rushed
through her, a joy that was just as suddenly dampened
when he informed her that he was going to the bar to
have a few drinks with some of the delegates. Nickie
nodded and decided to return to her room, since most of
the others seemed to be leaving.

Before getting ready for bed, Nickie sat at a small

table in front of a window overlooking the grounds and jotted down the names and identification of the people whom she had met, along with some questions she wanted to ask them. Then she opened the window, turning off the air conditioning to bask in the cool, fragrant night air as she undressed. Once she was in bed, the muffled roar of the distant ocean was a lullaby singing her to sleep.

Her slumber was deep and dreamless. Vaguely, she heard a phone ring in the distance, but the shrill sound only made her burrow more deeply into the pillows until she was jarred into semiconsciousness by an insistent knocking on her door.

"Nickie," called a resonant voice. "Wake up, sleepy-head, and let's go for a swim!"

"What?" Nickie shook her head, trying to remember where she was. A renewed knocking sent her stumbling to her feet. She pulled on a robe and went to open the door.

Rob smiled at her, amusement on his handsome face despite the look of concern in his brilliant eyes. "I tried to telephone you. When you didn't answer..." He looked at her closely. "Do you always sleep so soundly?"

"Not usually." Nickie yawned and rubbed her eyes. Blinking, she saw that he wore a pair of yellow swim trunks with a matching terry robe and was carrying a towel. "It must be the sea air. What time is it?"

"Seven-thirty." He grinned. "I'm an early bird..."

"Who gets the worm! Do you want to talk now, before breakfast?" she asked hopefully.

He laughed, although a faint annoyance showed in his face. "I thought you might like a swim."

Nickie hesitated, eyeing him suspiciously and trying to organize her thoughts. She wondered how he could possibly be so bright-eyed at such an early hour.

"We can talk if you want," he added lightly. "The first meeting isn't until nine."

At last she would be able to get some information

from him—it was too good an opportunity to miss. "Five minutes?" she asked.

At his nod, she closed the door firmly. Actually, she needed less than five minutes to slip into her bathing suit, a canary-yellow bikini, and pull on a long T-shirt dress. Taking a towel, she walked across the hall where the open door of Rob's suite beckoned. Her mind was still only half awake, and she longed for a cup of strong coffee, but she was determined to seem as alert as Rob.

Apparently, she was unsuccessful, for, seeing her, he said, "Come on, Sleeping Beauty," and led the way to the elevators.

Nickie followed silently. She paused at the pool where the lounges were still stacked to one side for the night; but Rob motioned her on to a path that led to the beach, which was deserted at that hour. The sun was already warm, with a promise of more heat to come later in the day.

"What did you think?" he asked, as he spread his towel out on the steep incline of the beach.

"About what?" Nickie replied, only gradually coming to life to appreciate the morning.

"About last night," he explained, seeming both amused and annoyed.

"Is there anybody you don't know?" she countered swiftly, brought awake by the tone of his voice. She still hadn't made up her mind about the previous evening, and she slowly spread out her own towel next to his and lay down, hoping to gain time.

"I doubt it," he answered smugly, raising himself on his elbows to look at her, obviously forgetting the subject at hand in his admiration of her slender body, which was already tanned from sunbathing on the roof. "You have sensational legs," he noted, running a light finger down one shapely thigh to her knee.

Nickie's skin tingled at his touch, and her breath shuddered in her lungs. She was all too aware of his trim body beside hers—the powerful chest matted with curly chestnut hair, the flat stomach, and the muscular arms and legs. "My legs have nothing to do with the conference," she retorted quickly.

"True," he said reluctantly, still looking at her. "We won't accomplish anything, you know. You heard it all last night: the Americans will talk self-help, and the others will talk interest-free or low-interest loans."

"Then why did you come?" Nickie asked, puzzled by the regretful yet cynical tone of his voice.

"Because"—he kept his eyes on her face, as if liking what he saw—"I keep hoping. I'm an optimist. I'd like nothing better than to put money in a local industry, if I could only be sure it would go to the people it's supposed to help—and not the capitalists and bureaucrats." Abruptly, he got to his feet. "Let's go for that swim, or would you rather stay here?"

Nickie dashed to the water behind him. The blue water that rippled invitingly in the cove was too tempting. Racing into the delicate, lace-fringed waves, she recoiled in shock at the coolness of the water before wading on and then plunging into it. She was fully awake now, paddling lazily in enjoyment. All thought of work fled as she watched Rob swimming beyond her with a strong Australian crawl that propelled him swiftly through the water. With a sigh of envy for his proficiency, she turned over to float on her back, closing her eyes against the golden sunshine and brilliant sky.

A splash nearby made her open her eyes. Rob, treading water, was watching her. His chestnut hair was water-slicked across his forehead, and his eyes were as vivid a blue as the sun-touched ocean. Nickie, thoroughly relaxed, smiled slowly at him.

Rob returned a lazy half-smile, his teeth white against the tan of his face, and stroked purposefully toward her. Nickie started to swim in the opposite direction, but was caught by an undertow. Before she realized what was happening, a wave lifted her up and deposited her into Rob's waiting arms.

"Don't you realize that some currents are just too powerful to resist?" he chided her, his arms tightening around her in a viselike grip.

She knew he wasn't talking about the water. "Rob . . ."

"Stop fighting me, Nickie," he murmured against her ear.

Helplessly, she looked up into his face. She knew the desire she saw there was reflected on her own traitorous features; she was breathing heavily, and her lips were parted in passion.

It was all the invitation he needed. His face bent to hers, and he captured her mouth with his own. She tasted the salty tang of the seawater and the sweetness of his full, soft lips as they stood together, locked in each other's arms.

The kiss lingered invitingly, sending a quiver of delight through her body. Nickie's senses, already aroused by the sun and the sea, gave way to the pleasure of the moment as their tongues met and explored each other's mouths. Not even the Caribbean and all its water could dampen the flame that leaped through her, lighting embers of joy in the very depths of her being.

Rob stood in the deep water with his legs spread and embraced her fiercely. Nickie's arms went around his neck, her body suspended under his. Her breasts rose, the nipples erect and straining against her bikini top and Rob's chest; her eager thighs met his.

He kissed her again, more urgently this time, crushing her mouth until she lost all sense of time and place and was conscious only of his sweet mastery. His body was light as air over hers. The cool, clear water was a cradle under a blue sky, and the sun was a molten gold. The kiss was filled with the life-giving elements of fire, water, and air.

Then he lifted his mouth from hers, and Nickie trembled with a deep sigh. Rob's eager lips were feather-light on her neck, then teasing and tantalizing on her breasts. Light-headed at the maelstrom of sensations he was arousing within her, Nickie pressed his head closer, her body arching upward to press against him with a fervor undiminished by the cool sea. Throbbing with renewed desire, she moaned softly.

A sudden wave rocked them, washing over her face and making her sputter. Her body tensed, and Rob gripped her more tightly.

He laughed. "Relax. I'm here."

As another wave broke, he began to pull her easily into more shallow water. Nickie breathed deeply, noting that Rob was completely in control. His arms were still around her, his blue eyes surprisingly tender.

With her toes digging into the sand, Nickie was re-called to reality. "I think I've had enough water for one day," she said, heading for the beach.

Rob followed and handed her a towel. Nickie took it, drying her body briskly, as if to rub away the glow inside her. What had just occurred between them in the water had left her confused and embarrassed.

She felt his eyes on her and looked up. He was grin-ning triumphantly—almost gloating, she thought.

"Water is your element, Nickie," he drawled slyly.

The kiss obviously meant nothing more to him than a casual conquest, and Nickie decided to act equally nonchalant. "We got carried away out there for a mo-ment," she remarked lightly. "That's all."

"Is it?" he challenged. "You seemed pretty . . . hungry for me a moment ago."

"Right now I'm hungry for breakfast," she said crisply, picking up her dress and stepping into it.

"Whatever the lady wants, the lady gets," he said with mock chivalry as he put on his robe. "Shall we adjourn to the terrace?" He held out his hand, but Nickie ignored it and marched past him up the hill.

Rob soon caught up with her, but made no attempt to touch her again or to converse. When they reached the terrace, he paused to greet some of the other participants who were already seated. Then he found a table and immediately summoned a waiter to order breakfast.

Putting aside the menu, he suggested, "Why don't you go into Willemstad later? Do some sightseeing."

"I'd rather go to the conference," Nickie replied. "That's why I'm here, isn't it?"

Rob smiled. "Today's meetings are closed to non-participants." He paused as the waiter brought their breakfasts. You might as well enjoy yourself."

Nickie bit her lip, deliberately pouring coffee from the pot the waiter had brought. "If I can't go to the meetings, when can we talk?" she demanded.

"There's a bus that leaves from the front of the hotel, or you can take a cab," Rob went on, ignoring her question. He began to eat, continuing to give her travel tips between mouthfuls. "Don't be fooled by the duty-free shops. If you know what you're buying, you can do pretty well; otherwise, prices are pretty much the same as in New York."

Nickie sighed and gave in, paying attention to her own breakfast. If the rest of the four days were going to be like this, she would find out little that would help her with the sample chapters Rob wanted her to write. He had been busy on the plane, and she had been too sleepy when they first came to the beach. It didn't help, either, that every time they were alone she became so enthralled by Rob Starr the man that she had difficulty seeing him merely as the subject of a biography.

"Finished?" Rob asked, breaking into her thoughts. "I'd better shower and shave. Do you want to stay here?"

"No." Nickie got to her feet, glaring at him. "I might as well go into Willemstad."

He grinned and took her arm. "You'll like it," he told her on their way through the lobby.

Nickie pressed her lips together, refusing to speak until they had reached their rooms. Unlocking her door, she said, "I'll see you later then?"

"Of course." Rob spoke blithely, although he looked at her with suddenly hesitant eyes. He opened his mouth, closed it, then said in a soft voice, "Have a good time."

Nickie closed the door behind her sharply. "Damn him," she muttered angrily, wondering if he was really serious about doing the biography at all.

While she showered and dressed, she tried to decide what she should do. Regardless of what she had said about Willemstad, she could always stay at the hotel and try to talk to Rob's colleagues—but they would be tied up, too. The best she could do was to conduct casual interviews in the evening at the rounds of scheduled cocktail parties and dinners. Rob would probably be furious, but in her present mood Nickie didn't care what he thought.

Dressed in a black-and-white cotton sundress and carrying a white jacket, Nickie went down to the lobby. Still brooding over a plan of action, she glanced uncertainly from the bus stop to the cab stand. As she did, she noticed a gray-haired woman of about fifty-five come out of the hotel. Nickie smiled, recognizing the woman as a Mrs. Naughton whom she had met, with Mr. Naughton, the previous evening.

"Hello, Mrs. Naughton," Nickie said brightly.

The older woman smiled in recognition. "You're the writer Rob Starr introduced us to."

"That's right—Nickie Monroe. Are you going into town? Perhaps we could share a cab," Nickie suggested, deciding to take advantage of the opportunity to gather information about her employer.

"Fine," Mrs. Naughton agreed. "I thought I'd take a cab to the Queen Emma Bridge and walk across to Willemstad. Otherwise, you have to drive to the harbor to take the bridge."

Nickie nodded. The other woman obviously knew her way around, and Nickie let her talk to the driver. She settled back in the cab, wondering how to bring up the subject of Rob without seeming too abrupt.

"These conferences are so boring," Mrs. Naughton said. "I come because my husband likes me to be here—and I love to shop. I had to keep reminding myself about the shopping last night during all those tedious speeches. They're always the same. One side asks for money, while the other tries to get the first to work for it." Mrs. Naughton shook her head.

"So Rob said," Nickie murmured, finding her opening.

"Really?" The older woman laughed. "I'm in good company, then. I take it this is your first conference?" At Nickie's nod, she continued, "Do you know Curaçao?"

"No. I thought I'd wander around a bit," Nickie admitted, trying to think of a way to bring Rob back into the conversation.

"Then let me show you around," Mrs. Naughton suggested.

"Thank you. It would be nice to have company," Nickie said with a smile. The more time she spent with Mrs. Naughton, the more likely she would be to learn something about Rob.

"That's settled then. I'm so glad we ran into each other." The older woman sighed. "These conferences do get lonely."

They had reached the Queen Emma Bridge, a narrow wooden structure at ground level that swung back to let ships pass on their way down the channel to the harbor. It swayed slightly as they walked across it, with Nickie admiring the Dutch-looking houses lining the channel. Except for their pastel pink and yellow and blue colors, they looked as if they would be more at home in Amsterdam than in the sunlit tropics of the Caribbean, where their stepped roofs seemed incongruous. The only white house—by law, Mrs. Naughton informed her—was Government House. According to the story, an early governor fresh from Amsterdam had stepped outside one morning and been blinded by the sun on the white houses; he'd immediately ordered them to be painted in colors.

As the two women wandered down narrow streets, stopping at a fish market on the banks of the channel and in the various duty-free shops where Nickie confirmed the truth of Rob's comment about prices, Mrs. Naughton chattered lightly. Nickie finally managed to steer the conversation to Rob's venture into Caribbean capitalism. By then, they were sitting under an umbrella in an outdoor café on the plaza, sipping iced tea.

According to Mrs. Naughton, Rob had given in to the pleas of the prime minister of an island whose only industry was tourism to start a small factory based on native crafts. The purpose was to help ease the chronic unemployment. As the requests for money had increased, Rob had asked for progress reports, but to no avail. Finally he had gone there himself, only to find the factory empty. The store had been filled with shoddy carvings imported from another island where the standard of living was so low that the artifacts could be produced there even more cheaply than in the factory. And even so, the shop was showing no profit, since the manager had managed to pad the payroll with friends and relatives.

"What did Rob do?" asked Nickie, beginning now to understand his cynicism.

Mrs. Naughton shrugged. Fanning herself with her hat, she said, "What could he do? He fired everyone and closed the operation down, taking the loss. The factory is still there, though, and he says that if a local entrepreneur would take it over he'd be willing to invest more money—but only after the factory proved itself."

"That seems generous," Nickie replied thoughtfully.

"He's a very generous man, even if that computer

executive from California doesn't think so. He claims that Rob cuts prices deliberately to drive him out of business!" Mrs. Naughton laughed. "If he did that as often as he's supposed to, Rob would be the one going bankrupt. Not even he can operate at a loss indefinitely." She smiled at Nickie. "Do you have time for lunch, or are you in a hurry to go back?"

Nickie agreed to lunch with alacrity.

"There's a good Indonesian restaurant on the channel," Mrs. Naughton suggested. "I like to sit there by the window and watch the ships go by."

"How marvelous," Nickie said enthusiastically.

The restaurant was on the second floor of one of the old Dutch buildings. It was cool inside, with its dark beams and high ceilings. They were seated at a white-clothed table overlooking the water, and Mrs. Naughton ordered the luncheon *rijstaffel* for both of them, as well as two beers, which she said was the only thing to drink with the meal, especially if the hot spices were added.

Nickie found out what she meant when curiosity tempted her to sample the three varieties of spices, their black, orange, and red colors denoting the range from mild to hot. Although each of the several dishes had an exotic flavor that appealed to her, she particularly liked the *saties*, small kabobs of marinated pork on wooden skewers, and the flat bread that seemed full of air and dissolved in her mouth.

Afterward, the women walked back across the Queen Emma Bridge to find another taxi to return them to the Hilton. They parted in the hotel lobby, with Nickie promising to meet the Naughtons for cocktails one night.

In her room, Nickie made notes on the information she had picked up and jotted down some questions she wanted to ask Rob. Then it was time to shower for the first cocktail party of the evening. As she was dressing in a simple black cocktail dress, the phone rang. To her disappointment, it was Rob telling her he was tied up and suggesting she go to the cocktail party and dinner without him.

By Thursday, Nickie was convinced that Rob was avoiding her. Although she had made it a point to awaken early, there were no more invitations for a swim. Nor did he show up at the beach, although Nickie went there every morning. She attended a few of the open sessions of the conference and all of the cocktail parties and dinners, gleaning a notebookful of information, none of which she had a chance to discuss with Rob, whom she saw only from across a room. Wistfully, she recalled that first morning, the delicious sensation of Rob's arm supporting her in the cool water, the taste of his salty lips on hers, the tremor of his body floating above hers. Occasionally, in a crowd, she would look around to find his eyes on her, seeming to caress her with the softness of his gaze, while a faint half-smile would make his lips curve invitingly. Yet he made no effort to approach her.

Nickie spent the last day on the beach. On her way back to her room, she stopped in the annex at the side of the hotel to look in the shops. A dress in one caught her eye, reminding her of the formal dinner that evening. She had planned to wear the gown she'd worn the first night, but one glimpse of the deep green chiffon dress was enough to tempt her to try it on. It made her think of a sari, the way the soft fabric was draped over one shoulder, leaving the other bare, to fall artfully as if molded to the curves of her body. When she moved, a faint gold thread shimmered through the material. She looked at herself in the mirror dreamily, the faint pulse in her temples beating more strongly at the thought of what Rob would think of her in the dress. She bought it impulsively, although it would make a noticeable dent in the money Rob had given her as an advance.

A message at the desk from Rob inviting her to his suite for cocktails made her even more pleased with her purchase. She took a leisurely shower and washed and conditioned her hair. Then she applied her makeup, keying her eyeshadow to the dress and thickening her lashes with mascara. Only a touch of blusher was needed to highlight her cheekbones. Finally, the dress was on, shimmering in the room's light. With her opera-length pearls and drop earrings, the effect was all that Nickie had hoped for.

Her full mouth curved in a smile, she walked across the hall to Rob's suite. He came to the door wearing a white dinner jacket and formal frilled shirt. When he took in Nickie's appearance, his eyes widened and a soft smile parted his lips.

"You look very special tonight," Rob said appreciatively. "Is it for me or for those old fogies you talk to every evening?"

Nickie laughed, her heart beginning to beat more quickly despite her determination to attend strictly to business. "If you won't talk to me," she said lightly, "what choice do I have?"

"Touché! I haven't given you much time, have I?" When Nickie smiled ruefully at the understatement, he promised, "I'll make it up to you. We'll have more time together in New York."

The intensity in his voice and eyes and the pounding of her heart made her want to believe him. She tried to avoid his lingering gaze as she shook her head. "I wonder . . ."

"Do you? I don't." The words seemed a promise, and Rob's mouth parted slightly as if in a prelude to a kiss that would seal the bargain.

The beating of her heart intensified. Nickie met his eyes, trying not to be charmed by the compliment in them. To her relief, a knocking on the door broke the mood.

"Damn," Rob muttered. He gave her a meaningful look as he opened the door for the Naughtons, whom he had invited for drinks.

Nickie smiled at the respite, happy to see Grace Naughton again. They were now on a first-name basis, and chatted like old friends. Shortly afterward, a few other people arrived. Nickie tried to listen to everything that was said, both over drinks and later when they moved to the dining room for dinner. Once again, Rob was seated on the dais, and Nickie in the back of the room. As soon as the speeches were over, she headed for Nils Claussen, the computer executive from California, first making sure that Rob was deep in conversation across the room.

"Mr. Claussen," she began, "I'm Nickie Monroe . . ."

The computer executive was a tall, heavyset man with icy, pale blue eyes under bushy gray eyebrows and a thin, tight-lipped mouth. "I know. You're the writer Starr brought with him," Claussen acknowledged. "What do you want from me?"

Nickie asked him about the conference, nodding sagely as he told her that it was a waste of time. "But you came here," she reminded him.

With what passed for a smile, Claussen said, "For the same reason your friend, Starr, did—to sell computers."

"Have you sold any?" Nickie smiled, looking at the man as innocently as possible to encourage him to talk.

"I hope so. This time"—Claussen smiled again—"you can tell your friend that I won't be undercut. I can drive him out of business as easily as he can me. The real money is in the programs, and I've hired the top Spanish-language programmer. Let Starr top that, because I can set my own price. He can't sell computers, however cheaply he makes them, unless he can sell the programs."

"You don't think very highly of him," Nickie commented.

"Why should I? He's a scoundrel, has been from the beginning with that tool-and-die company, buying out competitors by driving them under. He's tried it with me, but it won't—"

"Hello, Claussen." Rob's resonant voice was pleasant over Nickie's shoulder. "Congratulations on hiring Mendez. He's a good man."

Claussen looked at Starr in surprise. "Don't try hiring him away from me. I've got an iron-bound contract with him." He stalked off, heading toward the bar.

"Well, Nickie"—Rob said, his voice taking on a hard edge. "Just what do you think you're doing, talking to that man?"

"Trying to get some information." Nickie raised her eyes and saw that Rob's face was set and hard, the lines at the corners of his eyes deeply drawn.

"I see." He put a hand under her arm. "Let's get out of here." Gripping her elbow firmly, he propelled Nickie swiftly from the room toward the elevators. In the long, molded skirt, she almost had to run to keep up with him.

"Rob!" she gasped.

He ignored her, maintaining his hold until they were in the suite. Then, closing the door, he leaned against it, as if to prevent her from walking out. "Well?" he demanded, his blue eyes sharp and intense.

All the frustration of the past few days, her anger at being ignored each time she tried to talk to him, boiled up in Nickie. She glared back, willing her heart to stop pounding as their eyes met. "Do you or don't you want the biography written?" she challenged him.

A faint smile twisted the corners of his mouth. "In all honesty, no. You know that—and you know I feel I have no choice."

"Well, I seem to be in the same position," Nickie told him levelly. "If I want to write the book, I have no choice but to speak to other people. You leave me no alternative, since *you* won't talk, won't answer my questions."

"I told you. When we get back . . ." He looked away, unable to meet her eyes or, it seemed, to counter her charges.

Nickie sighed. Much as she could use the money,

even twenty-five thousand dollars seemed too little compensation for the frustration this project was causing her. Worse, it was clear that the more time she spent with Rob, the more difficult she would find it to resist his sensual appeal.

"If you want my opinion," she finally said, "I think you should forget the book. I can't write it this way. No one could. Unless you have something more to say, I'd like to go to bed now."

She put her hand on the doorknob, waiting for Rob to move away from the door. Instead, arms crossed, he stood his ground and met her eyes again, his dark brows knit together in puzzlement.

"You mean that, don't you?" he asked, apparently surprised that she was turning him down. "What if I offered you more money?"

Nickie laughed. "I wouldn't take it. It wouldn't be right, since I can't give you a book to show for it. Now, may I please—"

"Not yet." He unfolded his arms, taking her hands in his. "You're right. I haven't been fair."

Nickie started to withdraw her hands, not sure that she believed him. "Rob..."

"Let's go out on the terrace. It's hot in here." His smile melted her resistance.

Nickie let him lead her to the terrace where the trade winds, cool with the flower-scented air, ruffled her hair. She shivered slightly, not from the breeze but from Rob's closeness. Thinking she was cold, he put his arm around her, drawing her close to his shoulder, his strength flowing through her trembling body. To her surprise, Nickie could feel his heart pounding as hard as hers.

In the moonlight his blue eyes were dark and unfathomable as he lowered his head, lips parted to seek her mouth. Nickie tensed as an anticipatory shiver ran through her. But when their lips met, her will to resist evaporated in the echoing of their hearts and the bliss of the moment.

His tongue probed gently until her lips parted to welcome
the sweet invader, and the kiss became more urgent,
searing her to the depths. On a wave of passion, she was
lifted to a planet beyond the stars where only Rob and
she existed, suspended in an eternity of desire. The kiss
seemed to go on forever, filling her with a white-hot
need as she surrendered to his mastery of her mouth.

Rob's arms encircled Nickie and drew her close. Her
breasts heaved and the nipples grew hard against his deep
chest, while her thighs trembled at the pressure of his.
Of their own accord, her arms went around Rob's neck,
holding him even closer in the ecstasy of the moment.
Her fingers tangled in his hair, and she reveled in the
masculine feel of the crisp, chestnut waves. New pleasure
cascaded over her as Rob fondled her body, stroking
gently from her shoulders to the small of her back until
she arched against him in sensual abandon.

His breath was warm on her cheek as the kiss ended
and his mouth sought her ear, his tongue tantalizing it
until a new wave of joy made her sigh with longing. He
nibbled at the lobe gently, his desire concentrated in his
eager, exciting mouth and the hands that caressed her so
expertly. Once more his breath teased her cheek, then
returned to her mouth to claim her once more with a kiss
that took her breath away. His tongue played a seductive
melody against the sensitive membranes inside her mouth,
as she yielded herself to ever greater pleasures in the
shelter of his muscled arms.

Overhead the stars twinkled, and a wisp of cloud
passed over the full moon. The trade winds blew gently,
wafting a tropical perfume like a blanket over them. All
of Nickie's senses were alive with the night, with the
molten desire that filled her entire being. She seemed to
be floating on a cloud with Rob, and she swayed in his
arms, weightless except for the longing inside her.

"Nickie, Nickie..." His voice was low, vibrating
with need.

He picked her up in strong arms, cradling her body as she continued to hug his neck, and he carried her inside In a few strides he was at the door to the bedroom.

Nickie's head whirled. Her body still on that cloud, craving release, but her mind was coming back to earth, breaking the trance her desire had spun. She drew a deep breath, reining in her senses.

"Put me down, Rob," she said firmly.

His arms tightened. His mouth nuzzled her neck, sending a fresh surge of longing to her core.

"Nickie . . ."

"No." The refusal was as much to herself as to Rob. She took her arms from around his neck, the sensation of weightlessness fading as he put her down.

They faced one another, and Nickie was momentarily disarmed by the tenderness on Rob's face, lighting his blue eyes and softening his mouth into a sensual curve. She steeled herself against it, recalling how Gregory had succeeded in using his virility to manipulate her. She would not make the same mistake with Thomas Robinson Starr, who seemed to be using his sexuality to avoid a confrontation over the book. Though an inner voice urged her to forget the biography, she knew that she would write it if only to prove that she could—to herself, to Starr, and, she had to admit reluctantly, to Gregory. But she would never achieve her goal if she let personal involvement with Rob cloud her judgment.

Rob was staring at her, as if puzzled by her expression. "I was out of line, wasn't I?" he asked, his voice husky with emotion.

"We both were." Nickie took a deep breath. "Now, what about the biography?"

Rob leaned against the frame of the bedroom door and crossed his arms, his vivid blue eyes studying her face. "I want you to write it, now more than ever." His voice was vibrantly intense. "Will you do it?"

"Will *you* do it? Will you talk to me?" Nickie asked,

trying to keep her voice level and not think about any hidden meaning in his words.

"I'll do my best to satisfy you." Once more, his words were filled with innuendo.

"Will you?" Nickie retorted, not expecting a reply. "Good night, Rob." She left quickly, her hand trembling so much that she could barely unlock the door to her room. The fire inside her had not been extinguished. The embers were still smoldering, and one touch from Rob would ignite them again.

Chapter Five

AT SEVEN O'CLOCK Friday morning, Nickie was packed
and ready to leave Curaçao. She'd spent a sleepless night
worrying about that scene with Rob, wondering whether
she'd made the right decision. She knew she wanted to
go ahead with the biography—provided Rob was willing
to talk as he had promised. The situation, after all, was
not the same as the one with Gregory. In fact, the tables
were turned in a way. Gregory had been the professional,
telling her what to do. But with Rob, she'd just have to
make it clear that she was in charge, that she was the
professional. If she did, there would not be a repeat of
the night before. As long as she was serious, he would
have to be.

Rational as her argument was, it did nothing to change
the way her heart reacted to Rob's presence. She tried
to convince herself that the temptation she had felt in his
arms was a momentary aberration, an infatuation clearly
attributable to his money and reputation, not to mention

the romantic setting. In the cold light of New York, she told herself, any desire would fade, especially as she got to know him better and the aura of mystery about him faded. For the sake of the biography, she must not lose her objectivity—and she must not let Rob distract her anymore with his kisses and the warmth of his arms.

The last decision was easier to make than to keep, however. When Rob came to her door a few minutes later, her heart gave an unmistakable thump at the sight of his handsome face and powerful body. She would have to be constantly on her guard in order to keep things from getting out of hand again.

"Are you ready to leave?" Rob asked. The easy smile on his face deepened as he looked at her with hooded eyes. For a moment, he seemed about to take her into his arms, but his hand dropped to pick up her suitcase instead.

Nickie nodded, not trusting her voice. Fortunately, in the flurry of checking out and getting into the waiting car, she was not required to say much. As for Rob, he seemed lost in thought, although his eyes returned to her face again and again, their expression enigmatic.

When they arrived at the plane, the steward was waiting. Within moments of takeoff, he served them a breakfast of scrambled eggs, ham, toast, and coffee. Nickie, disturbingly aware of Rob's presence, gave her attention to the meal as she struggled to form a strategy. Rob ate quietly, too, watching her intently.

He finally smiled, his mouth curving sensually as he broke the silence between them. "What would you like me to talk about?" he asked mildly, although Nickie detected a twinkle in his eyes.

The question persuaded her that she had won her point the night before. She smiled her satisfaction that he was willing to talk, but just to be sure, she asked, "Then you're really serious about the biography?"

He shrugged, finishing the eggs and the last piece of

ham. "I said I would talk, didn't I? Fire away with your questions."

Nickie took a deep breath. "Why don't you start by telling me about your childhood?" she suggested.

"Just talk, you mean? Aren't you going to ask me any questions?" He seemed puzzled.

Softly and encouragingly, Nickie said, "I can't ask questions until I know more about you. Don't worry, I'll interrupt if I want to know more."

During the rest of the flight, Rob talked more freely than Nickie had expected. He told her that his father's sister had cared for him after his mother's death, and he'd rarely seen his father. His primary interest at Exeter, and later at Princeton, had been sports. He had excelled as a quarterback in football, and a pitcher in baseball. At the time his father died, he added, he had been considering offers from both professional football and baseball teams.

"Would you really have turned pro?" Nickie asked curiously, more fascinated than she wanted to admit.

"Sure. I'm a natural competitor, and the idea intrigued me." He laughed self-consciously. "I sometimes wonder whether I would have made it, but now I'll never know." He leaned back in his chair, linking his hands behind his neck and seeming thoroughly at ease. He flashed her a conspiratorial smile as his eyes met hers.

"Baseball or football?" Nickie continued quickly, steeling herself against the unsettling sensations his glance aroused in her. She bent her head, studying her notes.

Rob spoke thoughtfully. "Football, probably. Of course, one's playing life is shorter, but the idea of spending several years in the minors before playing big-league baseball didn't appeal to me."

"You sound like a 'young man in a hurry,'" Nickie mused, more to herself than to him. After listening to Rob talk, she was aware of a new dimension to him. Her heart had gone out to the lonely only child, cared for by a widowed, elderly aunt who did not especially like little boys, with an invisible father. A naturally gregarious child, he had doubtless channeled his desire for love into competitive sports to win the approval and praise from his peers and coaches that he never received at home. With that background, Nickie could understand how the same drive had led to a hunger for success and acclaim in business.

"I was . . . am . . ." Rob sat up, looking at Nickie pensively. "You know," he said in a surprised voice, "I've never told anyone that before. You're an even better interviewer than Louise said."

"I'm flattered," Nickie replied sincerely, a warm glow spreading through her body at the expression in his eyes and the sound of his voice. She fought her emotions, warning herself to keep her mind on business. "You see," she said, as lightly as possible, "it's not so hard to talk once you get started."

Rob laughed. The dropping of the wheels on the aircraft made him look out the window. "We're almost at Teterboro. We must have had a good tail wind. It was a short flight."

Nickie smiled, amused. According to her watch, the flight back had actually not been much shorter than the one down. The difference was that time had passed more quickly for both of them. What was more, for the first time, she was sure about the biography, sure it could be written and that Rob would cooperate. Still, she would feel more secure once she had gone home and sat down at her typewriter to put into words what she'd just learned from Rob. But first, she would have to transcribe her notes, which would take time, and phone some of the people whom he had mentioned to double-check his memory and impressions. She had at least a week's work in front of her, a week in which she knew she would have to stay away from Rob in order to keep him from influencing what she put down on paper . . . and to keep her mind on her work.

When they were settled in his limousine, which had been waiting at the airport for them, Burns at the wheel, Rob said, "Okay, Nickie, what next?"

"I'll type up my notes . . ." she began.

He waved an impatient hand. "I mean, what do you want to know next?" Now that he had started talking, he seemed impatient to get on with the project.

"I'll have to think about it. First let me write up what we've already discussed." She decided not to mention the phone calls she planned to make, feeling certain that he would take offense. He would not understand that what she really wanted was to add dimension to his story, not to challenge his own version of himself. And there was no point in proceeding before Rob had given her the official go-ahead. Until he approved the sample chapters, the biography was still in a kind of limbo and so was she.

He glanced out the window. He had told Burns to take Nickie home first since she lived closer to the Holland Tunnel. The car had left the tunnel and was turning north on West Street where the elevated West Side Highway had once stood. He looked with distaste at the ramshackle piers lining the river and the ancient, rundown buildings. When the car stopped in front of the loft building on Hudson Street, he said in disbelief, "You don't live here?"

"Oh, but I do. The building has been made over into apartments. It may not be Park Avenue, but it's home," Nickie joked lightly, opening the door of the limousine.

"It can't be very pleasant at night," he went on, seeing the empty factory buildings and the old storefronts, dotted here and there with a less than prosperous looking coffee shop or delicatessan.

"It's home," Nickie insisted, trying to deny to herself

that the neighborhood did look rather dingy and disreputable after the taste of luxury she'd just had.

"I'll see you up to your apartment." Rob got out of the car and took her suitcase from Burns. "Wait here," he told the houseman.

"It's not—" Nickie started to protest.

"Necessary," Rob finished. "I know."

Nickie pressed her lips together to keep from making an angry retort, convinced that the major motivation for Rob's gallantry was curiosity about where and how she lived. Well, she had nothing to be ashamed of, she thought, leading the way to the elevator that seemed to creak and groan even more than usual.

Rob eyed the decrepit cage skeptically and seemed relieved when it reached the fifth floor and they got out. Nickie, anger rising at his barely concealed disdain, quickly unlocked the door and reached for her suitcase. Rob ignored the gesture, brushing past her to enter the apartment. Nickie followed, anger fighting with self-consciousness over the bare walls and secondhand furniture.

"Would you like a cup of coffee?" she offered politely, wishing she had at least a bottle of wine in the house.

"No, thanks." He put down the suitcase and walked to the windows overlooking the roof, as if comparing it with his elegant penthouse terrace on Park Avenue. "Why don't you stay with me while we're writing the book," he suggested.

"You don't have to feel sorry for me," Nickie retorted, her pride flaring up. "I like it here."

"Do you?" Rob smiled faintly in disbelief.

Nickie was infuriated by his condescension. "I need my privacy when I write," she declared. "I couldn't work with you peering over my shoulder." She stalked past him to the door to the roof and opened it. "It's stuffy in here." A blast of hot air, smelling faintly of tar, reminded her of the sea breezes and the floral-scented air of Curaçao, and she turned her back resolutely on Rob.

"Nickie." His voice was gentle, but his grip on her shoulders was firm as he forced her to face him. "You don't even have an air conditioner." He looked at the high ceiling and the skylight. "Not that it would do much good. How *can* you work here?"

"I can. I do." Nickie's eyes met his, and her mouth trembled, parting slightly. His touch had started her heart pounding again with the desire she had vowed to resist.

"Why do you have to be so stubborn . . . and so beautiful?" he murmured, drawing her close to him, his lips brushing her forehead.

She pulled away and glared at him. "Beautiful? Stop trying to manipulate me with your phony compliments! Don't you realize I've seen the society-page photos of you with glamorous actresses and gorgeous debutantes?" The image of Joan Weldon, a svelte blonde with a Botticelli face as different from her own elfin features as night from day, flashed into Nickie's mind.

Rob stared at her, speechless. Then his look of amazement gave way to a tender expression. "Nickie," he said softly, "you've got me all wrong. You seem to equate beauty and glamour, but I don't. In fact, that first time I saw you on my terrace, I was struck with how real, how adorable you looked, with those huge, waiflike eyes, that pixie face. You were like the girl next door I'd always wished for as a boy. And since I've come to know you—your spirit, your utter unpretentiousness, your quick intelligence, your sweet singing voice . . . Don't you see that these things are part of beauty, too?"

"I was warned you were a charmer," she told him, resisting the sweet spell of his flattery. "But just because you have a way with words doesn't mean they're sincere."

"You underestimate your powers," he said. "But if words won't convince you of my sincerity . . ."

In one swift movement, he took her in his arms, crushed

her to his chest, and brought his lips down on hers. His mouth was like a fiery brand, and against her will desire surged through her body like the pounding of the sea. Her breasts rose against the granite wall of his deep chest, and she felt her nipples grow hard and ripe. Rob's hands glided down to the taut buds and gently teased them with his fingers, awakening a soul-shattering response within her. His practiced lips and hands were urging her to soar with him to the heights of ecstasy.

The passionate kiss ended, but Rob's lips found new pleasures in kissing her cheek, the tip of her nose, her eyelids. "Still doubt my sincerity, Nickie?" he murmured against her ear, the proof of his arousal straining against her trembling thigh.

"I don't know what to believe anymore," she gasped, giddy with the intoxication of his glorious male scent, his overpowering virility.

"I want you, Nickie. Come home with me. The book will go much more quickly at my place, and you'd have me at your command," he enticed.

At *her* command? No, he'd have her at *his* command. Dredging up all her instincts of self-preservation, Nickie reluctantly extricated herself from his embrace.

"It's no good, Rob," she said. "I won't come to Park Avenue. I don't want to come. And I won't be pressured into changing my mind."

Rob ran a hand through his hair in a gesture of frustration. "I guess I have to accept your verdict . . . for now," he conceded. "When will I see you? I mean, when will I see what you've written?"

"I'm not sure. It may take me a while to get something on paper," she cautioned. "What's your schedule?"

"I have to check with my secretary. Call me tomorrow." He looked around the loft again, shaking his head. "I repeat, I don't know how you can work here when you have the chance to—"

"Don't worry." She tossed her head defiantly. "I'll get the book done."

"I believe you. Remember, though"—his eyes glinted darkly—"I'm ruthless. I always get what I want."

When he had gone, Nickie sighed and picked up her suitcase. Her problematical relationship with Rob called to mind an anecdote Grace Naughton had told her about the orange liqueur for which Curaçao was famous. Originally, the orange trees had been imported to provide fruit, Grace had said, but the oranges had turned out to be quite small and too bitter to eat. Only by accident had someone learned they could be distilled into a deliciously sweet liqueur. Perhaps her relationship with Rob was like that, Nickie thought, moments of tension that distilled into the sweetness of a kiss that even now made her heart beat furiously with desire.

Chapter Six

OVER THE NEXT two weeks, Nickie would have lost all sense of time had it not been for *The New York Times* that she bought daily. Although she had never paid much attention to the business section, she now found herself studying it carefully for any mention of Thomas Robinson Starr, the Starr Corporation, or the various companies that came under the Starr umbrella.

She had spoken to Rob only twice since Curaçao. When she'd called the day after their return to ask him about his schedule, he had told her he would soon be going to Texas, where some exploratory oil wells were being drilled on leases he owned. Before he left, he had telephoned her to renew his invitation to stay at the penthouse, pointing out that she would have it all to herself. Nickie had been tempted, not only because he would be away but also because an unseasonable heat wave had made the loft stifling. Yet she had refused the offer again, knowing that if she did move in then it would be difficult to move out when Rob returned. He had not asked about the book, nor had he seemed particularly interested to hear that she would have the first few chapters ready shortly. There had been a pause before he'd promised to call her on his return.

In the meantime, she had spoken to Louise, who had urged her to get at least two chapters done as quickly as possible so they could be shown to a publisher. "I've been hearing all sorts of rumors about Burton Shields's book, Nickie," Louise had said. "As soon as you have even a draft, let me know. Interest is high, and the sooner I have something to show, the more I'll be able to get for it."

Nickie sighed as she rolled the last page of Chapter Two out of her typewriter. After going over her notes, she had called some classmates of Rob's at both Exeter and Princeton and had gotten in touch with his athletic coaches. From them, she had been able to draw a picture of an all-round athlete, competitive enough to be a one-man show except for his ability to inspire teammates. As one coach had said, "Robbie wasn't above 'hot-dogging,' but he did it to scare his opponents, not to impress his teammates." Just as he tended to do in business, Nickie thought, which was why she had ended the chapter on his college years with that quotation.

She was about to call Rob's apartment to find out when he was due back, when the phone rang. For a moment her heart pounded hopefully, and she picked up the receiver in anticipation of hearing his resonant baritone. Instead, a woman's voice said, "May I speak to Nickie Monroe, please?"

Nickie frowned at the slightly familiar voice with the faint New England accent. "This is she."

"Oh, Nickie, it's Grace Naughton..."

"Grace, how are you?" Nickie smiled, genuinely pleased by the unexpected call.

"I'm fine. And you?"

"Too busy to be anything but good," Nickie told her with a laugh.

Grace joined in her laughter. "In that case, I hope you're not too busy to come to a party on the Fourth of July. John and I usually go to the country, but this year we decided to give a party here. Why have an apartment with a terrace if we can't enjoy the fireworks on the East River at least once!" Grace exclaimed.

"I'd love to come," Nickie agreed enthusiastically, realizing the Fourth was only a few days away. In her rush to finish the two chapters, she had actually forgotten about the holiday.

"Good. I think you'll like the other guests. We'll be having cocktails at about six, and then a buffet—all very casual," Grace said.

Nickie repeated the time and jotted it down on her calendar before saying good-bye. As she got up and stretched, rotating her shoulders, which were stiff from the typing, she thought that the timing of the invitation was ideal. Now, if only Rob would get back and okay the chapters, she could go to the party in a more relaxed frame of mind. But a call to Burns informed her that Rob would not return until the Fourth at the earliest.

Nickie sat down again, glancing at her notes. Before going on, she really should talk to someone at Starr Tool and Die. Were it not for Rob, she would call the company now—but she didn't want him to think she was going behind his back. Besides, she needed to talk to someone who had been with the company at the time of his father's death, and she had no idea who, if anyone, would still be there eighteen years later. She would ask Rob about that if he liked the sample chapters, she decided. In the meantime, at least she had two good solid chapters completed. Perhaps the best thing to do would be to send them to Louise, whose judgment she trusted, for the agent's opinion and remarks. If Louise, as an expert, had no criticisms, how could Rob raise any objections?

Nickie gathered the pages together, eager to have them photocopied and in the mail before she could change her mind. Quickly, she addressed an envelope to Louise and hurried out, keys and wallet in the pocket of her blue jeans.

It was about four, the streets suffocating in the heat and seeming to shimmer in the bright sunlight, but Nickie barely noticed in her exhilaration at having finished her work. Her only regret was that she couldn't show it to Rob right away. She opened the door to the copier's, enjoying the fresh blast of cool air. Despite the uncertainty, her thoughts skipped ahead to the next chapter— the metamorphosis of the star athlete into the world-famous tycoon.

The more Nickie thought about that change, the less able she felt to account for it. She was still pondering the matter on the Fourth, as she took the subway to the Upper East Side. It was another scorching day, and Nickie had selected from her wardrobe a cool white cotton dress with a halter top and a multicolored striped jacket. Yet despite the light dress, she was hot and sticky as she left the subway at Sixty-eighth Street and Lexington Avenue. From there, she had to walk one block east to Third Avenue and then a few blocks north to the large, old-fashioned luxury building where the Naughtons lived, not far from Rob.

A maid answered her ring and showed her through cool, darkened rooms furnished in old-fashioned elegance, and out onto a large terrace. On the terrace, Nickie had to blink to adjust her eyes to the sunlight again. About fifteen people were there, the women dressed in summer silks and the men in slacks with dress shirts and ties. She spotted Grace standing near a bar at one end of the terrace. The older woman, in a sleeveless pink linen dress, saw Nickie at the same time and waved to her.

Nickie smiled and walked to the bar. "How good to see you again, Nickie," Grace said warmly, taking her arm. "You remember John; and this is my son, Jack." With her other hand, she drew a handsome fair-haired man about Nickie's own age toward her. "Jack, I'd like you to meet Nickie Monroe."

Jack acknowledged her with a friendly smile. "May I get you something to drink, Nickie? Something long and cold?"

"Vodka and tonic would be fine, Jack," Nickie told him.

"How's your work coming?" Grace asked. "You said you were busy, and I know you're a writer. What are you working on?"

Nickie hesitated, not sure she should talk about the biography—partly because she thought Rob might not want her to, and partly because she was superstitious about mentioning it until she had a contract.

"Don't be so nosy, Mother," Jack answered for Nickie, as he handed her a frosty glass. "I would imagine writers don't like talking about their projects. Is that right, Nickie?"

"In a way. Actually, I don't feel at liberty to discuss the project I'm involved with right now. As you know, I'm working for Rob Starr . . ."

"Oh, so that's it! I assumed from what he said at the conference that you were writing some publicity material for his firm. But apparently it's more than that?" John Naughton chuckled. "Never mind, Nickie. I won't pry. Knowing Rob, I'm sure there are good reasons for the secrecy."

Nickie was quick to take advantage of this opportunity to garner more information for the book. "You've known Rob a long time, haven't you, John?" she said.

He nodded. "Since he first took over at Starr Tool and Die. The bank I was with then was one of the executors of his father's estate. I'll never forget the first day I met Rob. He was barely twenty-one."

Nickie nodded, listening as John Naughton told her how both the bank and the management of Starr Tool and Die had been convinced that Rob would sell the business in order to pursue a career with baseball's New York Yankees or football's Green Bay Packers. When he had instead elected to run the firm, the initial reaction had been one of dismay. At first, Rob had had to prove that he was more than just a "jock," but within six months he'd won everyone over with his quick intelligence and keen business instincts.

"You know," John Naughton went on, "everyone— almost everyone, that is—accused him of trying to drive Bach Tool and Die into bankruptcy. Actually, it was the other way around. Bach made an offer to Rob to buy him out. It was so low that it was ridiculous, but Bach figured Rob was such a kid that he didn't know what he was doing. When Rob refused the offer, Bach lowered his prices to force Rob to meet them. It might have worked with someone else, but the maneuver only served to get Rob's dander up. He wasn't used to losing, still isn't, so he 'hot-dogged' it, in his own words, lowering prices to a bare break-even point. Bach panicked and tried to undercut him again, but Bach wasn't in as strong a financial position. The result was that Rob made him an offer and he was forced to sell. It took guts for Rob to do that before he was twenty-five. After that, there was no stopping him."

"Really, John, I hardly think Nickie's interested in ancient history." The voice behind Nickie was good-humored, and her heart skipped a beat at the familiar resonance.

"Why, Rob," she managed to say, turning around to see his handsome face, tanned to a deep bronze from the Texas sun, smiling at her. He was wearing an elegant white silk and linen suit that made him look like an ad in *Gentlemen's Quarterly*. "I thought you weren't due back until tomorrow."

"I couldn't miss Grace's party, could I, Grace?" Rob smiled at the older woman. "You should wear pink more often," he observed.

Grace flushed a pale pink to match her dress. "Why, thank you, Rob."

"Hello, Jack, haven't seen you in quite a while," Rob acknowledged the younger man affably.

To Nickie's surprise, Jack's only response to this friendly greeting was a curt nod. Apparently, he didn't share his father's admiration for Rob. Indeed, Nickie detected signs of hostility in the look Jack gave the older man, and she made a mental note to find out what that was all about as soon as she could manage some time alone with Jack. He gave her the opportunity almost immediately, taking advantage of a break in the conversation to remark, "There's dancing in the living room. How about it, Nickie?"

She glanced at Rob, who sent her an amused smile that she found disconcerting. She realized suddenly how much she had missed him and had looked forward to seeing him again.

"Go ahead, Nickie," he urged her indulgently. "I'll see you later. I want to talk to John for a minute."

She nodded and let Jack lead her off to the living room, where they joined several other couples who were taking a turn around the parquet floor to soft music on the stereo.

"You dance beautifully," Jack complimented her after a few moments of silence between them.

"It's just that you're easy to follow," she said graciously.

He gave a modest laugh. "Dancing is about the only exercise I get these days. They keep me pretty busy with paper work at the Legal Aid Society."

"You're not a banker like your father?" she questioned.

"No, I'm a public defender. Somewhat to my parents' chagrin, I'm afraid," he added. "They were pleased when I decided to go to law school, but that was because they expected me to take a job with one of the big corporate firms when I graduated."

"Oh, but your parents don't strike me as being snobbish," Nickie protested. "After all, I'm not exactly rich or famous, and yet they invited me to this party."

"Ah, but with a writer one never knows. Fame and fortune may be just around the corner for you, and they'll have known you when," Jack said cynically. "Besides," he continued, "you're a friend of the great Thomas Robinson Starr." His face darkened.

Here was her opening. "I gather you don't consider Rob a friend of yours," Nickie said bluntly, hoping he would reveal his reasons for disliking Starr with no further prompting.

Jack was silent for a minute. Then he asked abruptly, "Are you in love with him?"

The question startled her. "Of course not; he's my employer," she said, hoping she sounded convincing. "Whatever gave you that idea?"

"You were hanging on my father's every word when he was talking about the guy," Jack told her. "And when Starr joined us on the terrace, you suddenly took on a certain glow. Look, I know it's none of my business, but whatever you say, I think he's more than an employer to you. And in that case, perhaps I'd better warn you about him."

"Warn me about him?" Nickie echoed. She was embarrassed and confused by Jack's observations, but she brushed these emotions aside for the moment in her curiosity to hear what else he had to say.

"This really isn't the place for a private conversation," Jack said, casting a glance around the now-crowded living room. "Look, why don't we get together for a drink sometime next week, and we can talk then."

"All right," Nickie agreed, disappointed that he wasn't going to elaborate any further for the time being, but agreeing that the party was not an appropriate place for whatever revelations he had to make. "You can give me a call when it's convenient—I'm the only Nickie Monroe in the phone book."

"I'll do that," he said. "In the meantime, shall we go back to the terrace and get something to eat?"

At the buffet table, Nickie saw that John Naughton was standing in line with Grace, and that Rob was not with them. Before she could glance around the terrace to locate him, Grace took her arm.

"There you are, Nickie. I hope Jack's not monopolizing you," she said. Her laugh belied any anxiety about it, and Nickie wondered if Grace had asked her to the party with a matchmaking scheme in mind. If so, the plan was doomed, for despite his good looks, Jack held no romantic attraction for Nickie, and she hadn't noticed any signs of such interest on his part, either. She was sure he had only asked her to dance to get away from Rob, and his manner of holding her on the dance floor had been somewhat formal and impersonal.

"I was just about to introduce Nickie to some of the other guests, Mother," Jack said, a slight edge to his voice.

"Oh, Jack, I was only having my little joke," Grace said defensively. She gave Nickie an embarrassed smile, as if to apologize for the family friction.

John quickly stepped in to smooth the awkward moment. "There will be plenty of time to make introductions over supper," he said. "Right now, Nickie looks as if she'd welcome something to eat." He handed her a plate.

"I hope you like lobster and roast beef," he said, indicating platters of these delicacies at the center of the table.

"Thank you, everything looks delicious," Nickie said honestly, helping herself not only to the lobster and roast beef but also to a shrimp and avocado salad, slices of baked ham glazed to perfection, and assorted side dishes as well. She followed the Naughtons to a large table where some of the other guests were already eating, and found herself drawn into the conversation almost immediately. Her table companions included some high-ranking colleagues of John's from the financial world, and other corporate luminaries with their wives, as well as neighbors from the Naughtons' luxurious apartment building.

At first, Nickie felt somewhat intimidated by the surrounding aura of wealth and status, but she found everyone friendly and genuinely intrigued to be meeting a writer. A few of the other guests even claimed to remember seeing her byline on magazine articles, and complimented her on her writing style.

As they ate, Nickie couldn't help but compare these people with their varied cosmopolitan backgrounds to the rather provincial people she had met at Gregory's literary soirées. Before *Decade* had brought him celebrity status, he had associated mostly with fellow academics from local universities, more than one of whom was usually accompanied by an adoring female graduate student. Gregory had been their hero, not only because of his position as an editor but also because of his short stories. The conversation had generally turned to Gregory's past accomplishments and progress reports on his upcoming novel.

Nickie had listened worshipfully at first, although she now realized that her worship had gradually turned to resentment. At the time, her contribution to Gregory's novel was well known and envied. Yet how little any of them had known Gregory. When, even before publication, the novel had been acclaimed and Gregory was in great demand on the talk-show circuit, he had dropped all his old friends, herself included, for a new set.

"Would you care for more champagne, Nickie?" John Naughton interrupted her thoughts. "Or perhaps some coffee and dessert? We're offering both of the traditional Fourth of July favorites: blueberry pie and strawberry shortcake."

"As I recall, the lady is partial to strawberries," said a deep voice behind her. She turned to see Rob, whose smile looked rather forced, hovering behind her chair.

"How about it, Nickie?" he asked her. "I was just going over to the buffet to get some dessert myself."

With a smile at the other guests, she rose from her chair. Rob took her arm with a proprietary air and strolled with her toward the buffet.

"And I came to this party specifically because Grace mentioned you'd be here," he grumbled. "You might as well have been on the moon, for all the chance I've had to be with you tonight."

"It's your own fault," Nickie retorted saucily, secretly pleased that he was put out, even if he was exaggerating the degree of his chagrin. "You knew where I was—in the living room, dancing with Jack."

"Yes, I had thought to cut in on him and dance with you myself," Rob said, "but I had to speak to John in private for a few minutes, and we went to his study. From there, I went to the living room to look for you, but you and Jack were nowhere to be seen. So I came back to the terrace and found you already ensconced at that large table with the Naughtons. You might at least have saved me a seat."

Nickie raised her eyebrows. "You talk as if I were your date at this party. Whereas in reality, I didn't even know you'd be here."

"Ah, but I knew *you* would be here—which brings

us back to square one." They had reached the buffet, and Rob dished out a generous portion of strawberry shortcake, which he handed to Nickie. "Sweets to my sweet," he said gallantly. He took another helping of shortcake for himself, then steered her to a small table for two slightly apart from the other tables.

"Perhaps the Naughtons will think I'm rude if I don't rejoin them," Nickie worried.

"I'll think you're rude if you *do* rejoin them," Rob said dryly. "And I'm your employer, so you don't want to get on my bad side."

Nickie sensed he was only half teasing. "You know, you really can't go around clobbering people into getting what you want from them," she said lightly.

"Are you implying I'm a caveman?" he said with a suggestive leer. "I must admit, you evoke rather primitive urges in me. Still, I can see from the glint in your eyes that any 'Me Tarzan, you Jane' approach is going to result in *you* clobbering *me,* so why don't you sweeten your temper a bit with some strawberries and whipped cream while I commandeer a bottle of champagne for us."

She opened her mouth to chide him for his arrogance, but before she could say a word he popped a strawberry between her parted lips, then wiped the whipped cream off his hand by sliding the sticky thumb and forefinger across her tongue in a sensuous manner. A delicious shiver coursed up Nickie's spine, and she found herself unable to do anything but laugh at his insolence as she chewed the sweet fruit.

She was still chuckling to herself when Rob returned with a bottle of Dom Pérignon and two fluted champagne glasses. After pouring the wine, he handed her one full glass and raised the other in a toast.

"To a long and successful collaboration between us," he saluted her in his lazy drawl.

"Not too long," Nickie amended. "I spoke to Louise

recently, and she's anxious to show something to a publisher as soon as possible. Fortunately, I was able to send her my two sample chapters fresh from the typewriter."

"Before I've even seen them?" He cocked an eyebrow at her over his champagne glass before taking a sip. "I ought to be furious, but somehow, with you sitting there looking as luscious as this dessert, I feel . . . other emotions." He took another sip of his champagne and then reproached her for not touching hers.

"John Naughton kept filling my glass at dinner," she explained, "and I'm beginning to feel the effects."

"Good," he said, grinning. "Just loosen up a bit more, and then I'll whisk you off to the living room for that dance you owe me."

"That's what *you* think! If I loosen up anymore, I'll be too unsteady on my feet even to walk, let alone dance."

"I'll support you," he promised slyly, linking his arm through hers and maneuvering so that their glasses were raised to one another's lips as in an old-fashioned wedding toast.

Feeling self-conscious, Nickie took a sip from Rob's glass and then disentangled her arm from his. "All right, then," she acquiesced. "If we're going to dance, I suppose we should seize the moment."

"I'd rather seize you," he said wickedly as he rose from his chair and practically scooped her up from hers.

There were no other dancers in the deserted living room, and the stereo had been turned off, the records put away.

"Perhaps we'd better go back to the terrace after all," Nickie suggested, but Rob's powerful arms drew her to him in a viselike grip.

"One dance." It was an order rather than a plea. "I'll even supply the music—an apt song comes to mind." With both arms around her waist so that she had no choice but to put her own arms about his neck, he began to dance with her, crooning softly into her ear:

"Today, while the roses still cling to the vine,
I'll taste your strawberries, I'll drink your sweet
   wine.
A million tomorrows will all pass away,
E'er I forget all the joys that are mine today."

Nickie had to admit to herself that the suggestive lyrics were uncannily appropriate, and suspected Rob of deliberately staging the scenario. He must have observed the unsettling effect he'd had on her with his rendition of "Drink to Me Only With Thine Eyes" on the flight to Curaçao, and his serenading technique was even more overpowering now, as he held her in his arms, lightly caressing the small of her back as they swayed together in slow motion.

"If there are other verses, I've forgotten them," Rob said, "but if you'll carry the melody, I'll improvise a harmony." Obligingly, Nickie began to sing with him, but after the words "I'll taste your strawberries," he stopped her mouth with his own for a long, infinitely sweet kiss. Their tongues mingled, still tasting of strawberries and whipped cream and champagne, and Nickie's arms instinctively tightened around Rob's neck as he pressed her against his long, lean length with a low moan. Memories of the beach in Curaçao drifted across her mind and once more she felt suspended in time and space, floating with Rob to some interstellar paradise where they were the only inhabitants.

The kiss finally ended, but Rob made the next line of the song, "I'll drink your sweet wine," the prelude to another joining of lips and tongues. Yet this time their blissful idyll was interrupted.

"Excuse me"—Jack Naughton's mocking tones cut through Nickie's reverie—"but if drinking the sweet wine goes on as long as tasting the strawberries did, you two will miss the fireworks."

Nickie abruptly broke away from Rob and whirled

around. Jack was leaning against the doorframe, an ironic smile playing about his lips as he looked at them. "Mother asked me to round up all the guests on the terrace," he explained, as Nickie and Rob stared at him in startled silence.

"We'll be out in a minute," Rob finally replied coolly, waiting until Jack had headed back through the French doors before escorting Nickie in the same direction. His arm firm about her waist, he said softly, "Don't let Jack's boorishness embarrass you, Nickie. Even as a kid, he had a chip on his shoulder a mile high, and he doesn't seem to have mellowed any. He's probably jealous— Grace has mentioned that he doesn't have much social life. A case of all work and no play, apparently."

"Jack told me earlier that his parents don't approve of his work," Nickie remarked, trying to cover her confusion.

"Nonsense," Rob said brusquely. "Grace and John are only worried that Jack joined Legal Aid to spite them rather than because it was what he really wanted. The fact is, I offered Jack a job in my firm's legal department when he was a senior at Columbia Law School, and he turned it down in a rather nasty way. Too proud to work for a friend of his father's, I suppose. But he wasn't too proud to bum around at his father's expense for a few years between college and law school. Finding himself, Grace called it, but boozing it up was more like it."

"Well, if he did so much playing then, maybe that's why he's all work now," Nickie remarked. She wondered at Rob's portrait of Jack as a childish, spoiled ingrate. Was it an accurate description, or did Jack really know something sinister about Rob, and did Rob fear he had already told it to Nickie? In the latter case, it would be shrewd of Rob to try casting doubt on Jack's credibility, Nickie thought. Her former curiosity about Jack's warning to her returned full-force.

She had no time to dwell on the thought, however,

for as they reached the terrace, the first gold and red fireworks were bursting against the background of the East Side skyline, and she gasped her appreciation along with the other guests. Nestled in the crook of Rob's arm for the next half hour or so, Nickie watched in awe as a simulated Nigara Falls of exploding lights filled the sky.

As a final dazzling array of pyrotechnics faded away, leaving the stars to their lonely splendor in the quiet darkness, she gave an involuntary sigh. Rob's arm tightened about her shoulder and he murmured, "The fireworks don't have to end for us, Nickie. When we kiss, the explosion inside me is more spectacular than anything we've seen tonight, and I know it's the same for you. Come home with me, tonight, love."

Her heart hammering inside her, she murmured, "Please, Rob, let's not start—"

"Start?" he interrupted. "We're well under way. The difference is, I want to finish what we've started, while you're obstinately resisting destiny."

"Destiny?" she queried lightly. "It's you I'm resisting. What I want to finish is the biography, and to that end, I'd better go home and get a good night's sleep."

"Then I'll see you to your apartment."

"That's really not necessary. You live so nearby."

"Nevertheless, I brought my car expressly so I could drive you home. Besides, how can you continue with the book until I've seen those sample chapters?"

"That's true," she conceded. "Perhaps I should give them to you tonight, and you can call me as soon as you've read them."

"Good idea. So you see, I really must take you home— to pick up the chapters. Shall we say good night to the Naughtons now?"

After thanking Grace and John for the lovely party, they left together. In silence, they walked to the corner, where Rob had parked his Mercedes.

"Why did you send those chapters to Louise without

my approval, Nickie?" Rob questioned as he turned the key in the ignition.

"She called me while you were away, Rob," Nickie explained. "She'd heard rumors about the Shields book and was anxious to see what you had to say."

Rob groaned. "Damn that Shields." He turned south on Fifth Avenue. "We'll take the transverse at Sixty-fifth Street through Central Park. That's probably the quickest." He paused. "Is that why you called Burns?"

"About Louise?" Nickie was puzzled. "Yes. Why did you think I called?"

Rob shrugged. "I thought maybe you had changed your mind about working at my place. It must be an oven in that loft."

Nickie pressed her lips together, staring out at Central Park in the moonlight. The tree trunks were dark and mysteriously shadowed, adding a note of peril to the sylvan scene. How empty the park was; the only visitors seemed to be the cars hurrying quickly across the transverse. Ninth Avenue, on the other hand, was filled with a medley of assorted pedestrians who seemed to be scurrying by in slow motion in the humid night. At Forty-second Street, the sidewalk was even more crowded, especially with women in very short hot pants and high spindly heels, but even they seemed to move slowly.

Rob glanced at Nickie. Taking one hand off the wheel, he reached across the gear box to take her hand. "I'm sorry if I hurt your feelings."

The touch of his hand had its usual electrifying effect on Nickie. In addition, she realized how much she had missed him, how she had enjoyed their brief dance, his sweet kisses, and his sheltering presence during the fireworks.

"That's all right, Rob," she said softly, as he parked in front of her building. "If you'll just wait here, I can get those chapters for you."

"Why don't I come up and read them now," he suggested. He smiled winningly. "To be honest, Nickie, I'm too curious to wait."

Nickie's heart leaped at the eagerness in his voice. For the first time, he seemed anxious about the book. Then, just as quickly, her heart plummeted. The book, Rob's book, had become important to her, far too important if his approval meant so much to her. She frowned slightly, dark brows drawing together. Rob locked the car after looking around carefully, then took her arm protectively.

Inside the apartment, she turned on the old wrought-iron floor lamps by the couch. Now that he was here, she was a little apprehensive about his reading the chapters. She wasn't sure he would like them, or the fact that she had called so many of his youthful associates. "Are you sure you want to read this tonight?" she said. "You must be tired."

"Now that I'm here, wild horses couldn't stop me," he assured her.

Nickie went slowly to the desk, picked up the photocopied chapters, and reluctantly handed them to him. As he settled down in a corner of the couch, she opened the door to the roof and turned on the fan in front of it. Although Rob hadn't complained about how hot it was in the loft, she didn't need him to remind her of the fact, not with perspiration beading her upper lip. The powerful fan soon did its job, however, cooling off the large room as much as possible.

Seeing Rob's eyebrows knit in concentration, Nickie's knees went weak and she leaned against the desk, watching him for a sign. He took his time, reading each page thoroughly before putting it down beside him, meticulously lining up the corners. Nothing in his face betrayed his thoughts, with the result that Nickie's apprehension increased until she almost stopped breathing. When he finally put down the last page, her lungs were bursting.

Exhaling a long sigh, she whispered, "What do you think? Is it? . . ."

Rob got to his feet slowly. "You certainly talked to a lot of people—and without my permission. But then, you've given me ample warning that you're headstrong and do things your own way."

"I had to do it, to fill in what you told me," Nickie explained anxiously, although she noted with relief that his blue eyes were twinkling.

Rob shook his head in wonderment as he approached her. Her heart began to beat more quickly, and she held her breath again in her eagerness to know what he was thinking. "It feels strange to read about yourself, to find out what other people think, say, about you." He put his arms around her, drawing her close until his cheek rested against hers.

The embrace, the warmth of his arms, and the faint scratch of his beard expressed Rob's feelings more clearly than words. The embrace was tentative and exploratory, and somehow this made it all the more seductive to Nickie. New York in July faded to a tropical island that was only now discovered. Rob and she were Adam and Eve in a brave new world.

Her spirit soared. She knew he liked what she'd written from the tender way he held her. She reveled in the closeness and the fit of his strong body, the deep chest resting against her breasts, the muscled thighs pressing hers. She rubbed her cheek against his, the faint tickle of his beard sending a wave of pleasure rippling through her.

"Nickie . . ."

A high-pitched screech interrupted whatever he was about to say. His body tensed alertly, and he raised his head, trying to sense a danger from which to protect her.

Nickie's breath caught as a laugh bubbled through her parted lips. The screech had been answered by another, almost human wail. "It's the cats from next door," she finally managed to say, her unfulfilled longing finding an outlet in the laughter.

Rob looked at her, obviously confused, before he sought the same release in laughter. The two cats, unaware of the wonder that they had broken, were soon joined in a chorus of feline caterwauling and passion. "Cats!" His voice was disgusted. "I thought someone was being murdered outside the window."

Nickie used the pause to gather herself together. Those blissful moments in Rob's arms had made her forget that the book was still at stake. Taking refuge in the deep chair behind the desk where she had spent so many hours, her body still weak and trembling with desire, she reminded herself that she was a writer, a hard-working writer, that Rob was merely the subject of her current work.

She took a deep breath. "You haven't told me what you think."

He studied her, one eyebrow raised in amusement. "I think you're desirable, passionate..."

Nickie could feel her face flaming. Though he sounded sincere, she was annoyed at the evasion that was so typical of his whole attitude toward the biography. "I was talking," she said, her voice strong and clear, "about the two chapters."

"Oh, that!" Rob waved a casual hand. "Well, you were right to send them to Louise. Of course, it's eerie for me to be reading the story of my own life, but I think I can be objective anyway. I have to admit that if I were a publisher, I'd want to see more. You certainly make me seem... well, fascinating."

Nickie smiled. "You *are* fascinating," she told him.

"Am I?" His eyes held hers in thrall for a moment, but the renewed cacophony of the cats on the roof broke the spell. Rob grimaced. "How can you sleep or work with those cats carrying on?"

"I hardly hear them anymore," Nickie admitted in all honesty.

Rob shook his head disbelievingly and took her hands in his. "Nickie, why don't you move into my apartment? I promise I'll leave you alone if that's what you want. You'll have your own room, a quiet place to work..."

Nickie glared at him. All her previous ardor threatened to erupt in anger at the reminder of Gregory's similar proposition. She opened her mouth to refuse.

Rob laid a finger on her lips. His eyes were both alert and tender. "Wait a minute," he said, as if sensing her objection. "How about a compromise?"

Nickie examined his face. His touch was exciting her again, despite the fact that she could not help but wonder what kind of a compromise he might have in mind. And her heart was beating faster at the thought that he was willing to find a middle ground, showing a sensitivity beyond stubbornness.

"I won't ask you to move in again...unless you want to," he added with a grin and a lifting of one eyebrow that was teasingly erotic.

"Then, what?" Nickie's own stubbornness weakened, although she could not imagine what he was driving at.

"All I ask is that you try working at the apartment. How do you know whether or not you can work there," he asked logically, "unless you give it a try?"

Nickie had no answer to the question. In a way, it would be like going to a job. Simply working at the apartment was not the same as moving in. In addition, undoubtedly he would not be there. The Starr Industries offices were on Wall Street. "I'll try it," she agreed softly. If he could compromise that far, so could she.

He smiled, taking his keys out of his pocket and removing one from the ring. "In case you need it," he said quickly, forestalling her objection that she would not need a key because of Burns.

"Then you do want me to go on with the biography?"

she asked, remembering that despite his praise of her writing, he had not yet committed himself.

Rob's indecision was both exasperating and touching. From the way that he pursed his lips thoughtfully, she knew that he didn't really want to go on, that he still didn't like the idea of it, but that he realized the choice was out of his hands. He was the kind of man, moreover, who hated to feel indecisive. He looked into her eyes. What he saw made his mouth straighten, as if his mind were made up. "Yes," he said slowly. "I'll have my lawyers draw up a contract and send it to Louise."

Nickie nodded and took the key. "I'll be there about nine tomorrow. Is that all right with you?"

"Fine!" Rob smiled, his eyes alight. He took her face in his hands, the palms gentle and seductive on her cheeks. Before Nickie could say anything, he murmured, "To seal the bargain."

His lips closed on hers. Nickie's heart beat with fresh desire at the touch of his lips. Once more, she felt she was being transported to that secret island known only to Rob and herself. The key was still in her hand, and she wondered if now that Rob had won one point, he was about to try to win another, regardless of what he had said about compromising. If the first kiss had won her concession to work in the apartment, did he think the second would convince her to move in?

She could not let Rob seduce her into losing her independence the way Gregory had. Her hand tightened on the key, as she forced the kiss to a close.

Rob looked at her quizzically.

Nickie smiled, trying to sound lighthearted. "It's late, and we both have to be up early—to go to work," she announced.

Rob didn't give up so easily. He put an arm around her shoulders to try to draw her into an embrace. "Tomorrow will take care of itself," he whispered, lowering his head for another kiss.

"It already is tomorrow, Rob," Nickie said firmly, evading his mouth.

He nodded slowly, his blue eyes darkening with desire, but he didn't protest anymore. A smile teased his lips. "I'll be waiting for you," he promised. His hand squeezed hers, and he gave her a soft kiss on the cheek, as if unable to resist it, before striding to the door.

Nickie followed, standing in the doorway of the loft to look after him. The elevator was still on her floor, and he blew her a final kiss before getting in and disappearing from view.

Out of sight but *not* out of mind, she thought ruefully. And though she determinedly concentrated on other things as she tossed and turned in bed an hour later, when sleep finally came, her dreams were haunted by a pair of lips that tasted of strawberries and champagne, and the compelling man to whom those lips belonged.

Chapter Seven

NICKIE RANG THE bell of the penthouse at nine sharp. She had no intention of using the key unless she had to. To let herself in was too reminiscent of her relationship with Gregory, of the way he had given her the key to the loft so she could "make herself at home" while she waited for him on those nights that he was delayed at work or the New School.

Burns opened the door so promptly that she knew he'd been expecting her. At the same time, his usually impassive face showed a glint of surprise at the sight of Nickie in what she considered to be her work clothes. To prove to Rob her intention of working in her own way, she had deliberately put on her blue jeans, a red T-shirt, and leather sandals. In addition, she was carrying an enormous saddle-leather shoulder bag, into which she had packed notebooks and other writing materials she thought she might need.

"Good morning, Miss Monroe," Burns said, a hint of amusement in his voice. "Mr. Starr is waiting for you on the terrace."

"Thank you, Burns," Nickie answered. Both his words and his expression fostered her premonition that she should never have agreed to work here, especially since her heart was already pounding in anticipation of seeing Rob again, most especially after the previous evening.

The handsome tycoon was reading *The Wall Street Journal* over breakfast. At the sound of her step, he looked up eagerly, his blue eyes vividly alight.

"Good morning," she said, her voice level but huskier than she would have liked. Recalling Burns's initial astonishment, she added, "As you can see, I dressed for work."

"So you did," Rob murmured, dropping his gaze from her face to take in her attire. As if he were determined to live up to his word about her being free to work, he visibly checked himself from rising to greet her, although he did not take his eyes off her.

"Well?" Nickie asked, trying to resist the weakness in her knees that the warmth in his eyes inspired.

"Well, you're just in time for breakfast," he announced, his face breaking into a brilliant smile. "What can Burns get you?" he inquired solicitously.

"I'd like some coffee—after you show me where I'm to work," she told him briskly.

"Have the coffee first—here," Rob urged, a teasing light in his eyes challenging her to stay with him on the pleasantly cool and shady terrace.

Nickie sighed. Actually, she wanted the coffee immediately. She had left the loft shortly after eight, walking to Eighth Avenue and Fourteenth Street to catch the crosstown subway to Union Square, where she had changed to a Lexington Avenue local that had inched its way uptown. Both trains had been hot and crowded with sweating rush-hour passengers, and she had considered going back home and calling Rob to tell him she'd changed her mind about working at his penthouse. No matter how hot the loft might get, nothing could be worse than being on the subway at rush hour in the heat of summer.

Rob took her silence for acquiescence and poured piping hot coffee from a silver pot into a waiting cup. Beside it, in a bowl of cracked ice, was a temptingly frosty glass of orange juice. Nickie smiled reluctantly and sat down.

When Rob grinned triumphantly, she stiffened. "By the way, where am I to work?" she asked.

As she spoke, she wondered why Rob seemed in no hurry to be leaving for Wall Street. Surely he wouldn't be going downtown without changing clothes, she thought, noticing that he was dressed as casually as she was—as casually, in fact, as he had been on the Friday she had met him—in a white polo shirt and gray slacks. Her misgivings grew stronger, and she picked up the glass of orange juice to give herself time to think.

Rob seemed unaware of what was going on in her mind as he said, "My secretary, Joyce, and Burns are fixing up the room next to Joyce's. It has a typewriter, a desk, everything I think you'll need. There's a door into the library, and you can pop in any time you have a question."

The orange juice was tartly refreshing, but Nickie almost choked on a swallow. Despite that initial interview and the fact that she hardly expected him to keep strict nine-to-five hours, she had somehow assumed that Rob went to Wall Street every day. But now she recalled his earlier comment about being at her command if she worked at the penthouse and realized he probably maintained an office here too. She had to say something, because Rob was staring at her, full of concern over the way she'd choked on the orange juice. "I . . . swallowed the wrong way," she managed to say. Then she blurted out, "Don't you ever go to Wall Street?"

Rob grinned. "Only when I have to," he said slyly. "As president of Starr Industries, I can pretty much run things from here. And I find each president of the individual companies works better if he feels I'm not breathing down his neck. My secretary can take care of any correspondence here as well as at Wall Street, and telephones and a teletype keep me closely in touch."

Nickie nodded, knowing she had only herself to blame for her assumption. "About a telephone. I'd like to make some calls."

"You mean you want to continue talking to other people about me?" Rob's mobile mouth thinned into a disapproving line.

"I must be able to talk to whomever I want, to write whatever I think best," Nickie reminded him, her own mouth set.

He backed down with a reluctant shrug. "The apartment has four lines. You can have one extension for your exclusive use."

Nickie nodded. "That would be great." She drank the coffee and put the cup down firmly. "Well, then, I'll get to work." She stood up, signaling her resolve not to be delayed any longer.

"Sure." Rob also rose. A faint smile twitched at the corners of his mouth as he took in the blue jeans and shirt once more. "I dreamed of you last night," he said softly.

Nickie's full lips parted slightly. Remembering her own erotic dreams, it seemed an eerie coincidence, until she decided that he was probably just saying it as a ploy to disarm her.

"I want to get to work, and I intend to do just that," she said staunchly, refusing to be distracted.

Rob grinned unabashedly. "I promised to let you work, didn't I? But you look so seductive."

"In old blue jeans?" She was frankly skeptical.

"In anything . . . nothing . . ."

"Where's the office?" Nickie asked abruptly, determined to end this dangerous conversation.

"This way." Rob gave her another longing look and then led her through the apartment to a small office behind the library. A smart-looking woman in her early forties who was busy at a typewriter looked up expectantly as they entered.

"Nickie Monroe, Joyce Slocum," Rob said, introducing the two women. He walked through the office to another door, adding, "Here's your office, Nickie. If you need anything, ask me—or Joyce," he put in quickly.

Nickie followed him into the office, a large room with a big desk and leather chairs. Next to the desk was the latest model electric typewriter on a stand. "I assume"—she nodded at the door on the opposite wall—"that leads to the library."

"Right." Rob half-sat on the edge of the desk, watching Nickie sit down behind it and start emptying her large shoulder bag. "You could almost get the 'kitchen sink' in there," he said conversationally.

She looked up and bit her lip. "Rob," she replied, strain evident in her voice, "if you won't let me work, I'll go home now."

"I'm sorry." He strode to the door. "Holler if—"

"Yes, I know. You or Joyce . . ." Nickie pressed her lips together, opening a drawer to find several kinds of paper in slanted compartments. She took out a sheet and rolled it into the typewriter, trying to ignore Rob. A softly closing door told her he had taken the hint and left, and her shoulders sagged with relief. Picking up a notebook, she frowned at her notes. Soon her fingers began to fly.

An hour later, as she paused to look over what she had written, the door to the library opened. When she glanced up, she found Rob watching her.

"I thought by the silence that you might be stuck and need my help," he explained hopefully. "Do you want a coffee break?"

"Okay," Nickie agreed, thinking that another cup of Burns's superb coffee would indeed by welcome.

Rob grinned and picked up the phone, pressing a button for the intercom and dialing 7. When Burns answered, he told the houseman to bring them coffee. "How's it going?" he asked Nickie.

"Pretty well." She leaned back in the chair, her mind more on the pages in front of her than on Rob himself. An idea came, and she turned back to the typewriter, fingers flying again, vaguely aware of Burns coming in and leaving.

"Here's your coffee," Rob said from behind her.

Nickie jumped, suddenly realizing that he had been reading over her shoulder. "You scared me!" she accused. "If you want to read, at least wait until I take the page out of the typewriter."

"I'm sorry." He sat down in a chair across the desk from her, looking so abject that she had to smile. He brightened in response. "I won't do it again, I promise." He crossed his heart to show his earnestness.

"You're forgiven—this time." Nickie stretched. She had done more work than she'd expected, part of the reason being that she was still dealing with Rob's early life. This was the easy part; it was like writing about a stranger. The Rob sitting across the desk, relaxed and in control, was unrelated to the driven, competitive, younger Rob. When had he changed, she wondered. Perhaps he had never really changed, only become more sure of himself, covering the drive with a veneer of assurance. More than once she had sensed how much he hated to lose. Yet this compromise—her working at his apartment but not living there—was proof that he could be flexible, to an extent.

Unexpectedly, Rob got to his feet. "I'm disturbing you, aren't I?" he asked softly, showing a sensitivity that surprised and pleased Nickie. "I understand," he continued as she looked at him wonderingly. "I'll go." At the door, he said, "I told Burns to serve lunch at twelve-thirty—in an hour and a half. Is that all right with you?"

Nickie was again touched by his considerateness. "That's fine, Rob," she agreed. As soon as he had left, she reached for the phone, suddenly remembering that she ought to call Louise about the first two chapters and to let the agent know where she was. Louise, however, was not in. Nickie left her name and number with the secretary. Then she called Information and asked if there was a listing for Henry Bach. Bach might not want to talk to her, but she ought to at least try to get his side of the story.

To her surprise, Bach seemed eager to discuss the takeover. He launched into a tirade of invective against Rob, obviously rehearsed from a previous conversation with Burton Shields. Under Nickie's questioning, how-ever, he confirmed John Naughton's version of the story—that he, Bach, had been the first to cut his prices, seizing on Starr's youth and inexperience and counting on it to provide a lever with which to force Starr to sell to him. When Rob had outmaneuvered him, he had not given in gracefully.

After thanking Bach for his cooperation, amused at how unwittingly he had revealed himself and not Rob to be the villain of the takeover, Nickie hung up the phone and went back to her typewriter.

The sound of the door opening some time later startled her. When she saw Rob looking at her expectantly, she asked, "Twelve-thirty so soon?"

"I knocked, but you didn't hear me," he explained.

Nickie smiled, once more noting his sensitivity. She felt an increased trust in him now, especially after her conversation with Bach. "Let's eat," she said softly, trying to ignore the flutter of her heart that his thoughtfulness had evoked.

He stood back to let her precede him, and she walked quickly to the terrace, intending to convince herself as

well as Rob that lunch was to be a business break and
not a social event.

From the way the skyline was shimmering as if under
water, Nickie knew the day was hot. Yet the air-conditioned office and now the terrace high above the street
were refreshingly cool. It was like being on the rim of
a canyon in the middle of nowhere, especially under the
umbrella table. Nickie sat down, breathing deeply of the
fresh air.

Rob had stopped by a portable bar under the lush,
potted trees. "Can I get you a Campari and soda?" he
asked. "It's a cool drink on a hot day." He had already
poured the red liqueur over ice in a glass and was adding
soda.

Nickie's initial relief at his keeping to the agreement
dissolved a little. Again he seemed to be delaying her—
from a quick lunch, this time. "I'd prefer iced tea," she
replied, although the sparkling ruby-red drink looked
appealing. "I thought you said lunch was at twelve-thirty."

Before Rob could reply, Burns appeared with a tray
bearing cups of vichyssoise garnished with fresh dill.
Next came rosy prawns in a tarragon-flavored vinaigrette
dressing with deviled eggs, a tomato-and-endive salad,
and crusty, warm garlic bread. It was a far cry from the
peanut-butter or egg-salad sandwich that was Nickie's
staple lunch. Best of all was dessert—a scoop of home-
made vanilla ice cream with chocolate sauce.

Nickie attacked her food with determination, hoping
to persuade Rob she was in no mood for idle chitchat.
He let her eat, watching her delightedly, his eyes warm
on her face. At the same time, he appeared surprised
when she pushed aside her empty ice-cream dish and
stood up.

"Where are you going?" he asked.

"Back to work," she announced firmly. "I don't usually take this much time for lunch." She glanced at her
watch. Nearly an hour had gone by. She'd found herself

unable to gulp the carefully prepared food, yet she hadn't realized just how slowly she'd been savoring each mouthful.

Rob laughed. "Well, now you've got someone to look after you, to see that you eat properly."

Nickie stared at him, taken aback by his words and his carelessly paternal manner. "Really, Rob, I can take care of myself!" She was sure that the idea of her moving in with him would come up once more.

"I've seen the way you take care of yourself. You deserve better than that," he insisted.

"It's a matter of opinion." Nickie looked around the large, beautifully landscaped terrace as a cool breeze bathed her cheeks.

"I won't argue the point now," Rob told her softly. He moved as if to embrace her, then stopped himself. "Go back to work, but think about what I said."

Nickie nodded, then hurried back to the office. As soon as she sat down, the intercom on her phone buzzed. She picked it up to hear Joyce's voice telling her that she had a call on line three. Nickie pressed the appropriate button on the phone.

"Nickie, it's Louise," the agent said in response to her hello. "I assume you called about the sample chapters, and I'm delighted to tell you that I think they're first-rate. In fact, I spoke to Richard Smalley about them, and he's very interested."

"Oh, Louise, that's wonderful!" Nickie exclaimed. Smalley Publishing Company was one of the most prestigious firms in New York.

"Wait a minute, Nickie," Louise warned. "I assume the chapters—and the fact that you're at Starr's—mean that he *is* going ahead with the biography. We'll need a contract."

"His lawyers are drawing one up," Nickie assured Louise.

"Good. You're also going to need an outline for the

rest of the book. Rob's obviously opening up to you about his life, but he's going to have to open up completely. I mean about Joan Weldon, of course."

"Of course," Nickie said with a confidence she didn't feel. "When will you need the outline?"

"Well, I sent the chapters over to Smalley by messenger a few minutes ago. He said he'd take them home with him tonight. Assuming he likes them as much as I do, he'll probably want the outline as soon as possible."

"I'll get going on it right away," Nickie promised.

"Good. Oh, there goes my intercom; I've got another call. Look, Nickie, phone me again when the outline's ready, will you?"

"Sure, Louise. Good-bye now."

True to her word, as soon as she had hung up the phone Nickie put aside the chapter she had been working on and tackled the outline. It took her several hours, but was easy enough to work up from her notes—except for the chapter on Rob's romantic life. Of course, she knew the names and something about the women Rob had been photographed with, but he himself—and perhaps even some of the women he'd dated frequently—would have to supply her with the personal details that would interest readers. And a major segment of the chapter would have to be devoted to Joan Weldon.

Nickie sighed. It was nearly five o'clock and she should be getting home, but she'd have to talk to Rob about the chapter on his love life immediately. She hoped he would be free—and willing—to discuss it with her tomorrow morning. She decided to start off by telling him about Smalley's interest in the book—Rob would be as fastidious about having a reputable publisher as he had been about getting a "responsible" agent. From there, she'd explain about the necessity for the outline, and then . . . well, she'd just have to play it by ear.

Opening the door to the library, she smiled brightly and said, "Rob . . ."

At one end of the capacious room was an enormous desk and an easy chair. In front of the desk was a large leather chair, while at the other side of the room were a matching sofa, a handsome marble-topped coffee table, and two other chairs.

Rob was sitting on the couch, a phone in one hand and what looked like a sheaf of legal papers in the other. As she hesitated in the doorway, he motioned her closer, a smile on his sensual mouth. The phone conversation must have been almost over, for he said, "That's it, then. Call me back if there's another problem." After he had hung up, he smiled more broadly at her.

"I didn't mean to interrupt," she said hastily, afraid he might think she was turning the tables on him.

"That sounds familiar. You look like the cat that swallowed the canary," he added with a smile.

Nickie laughed. "I didn't swallow all of it. I saved half for you. Louise likes the sample chapters. She's sent a copy to Richard Smalley, who's expressed serious interest in doing the book."

"I see. Come here, Nickie." He patted the couch.

She hesitated, then obeyed his request and sat down next to him. "Aren't you pleased about Smalley?" she asked, nervously twisting the typed outline in her hands.

He gave her a wry smile. "In all honesty, I'm more pleased for you than for myself. You know my feelings about the biography are still ambivalent, but this would be quite a coup for you. If Smalley publishes the book, there should be no problem getting him to look at your novel, right?"

Nickie was startled. "What do you know about my novel? You've never mentioned it."

"Neither have you. Actually, all I know is what Louise told me—that you've started writing a novel and you need money to live on while you complete it. Do you want to tell me more?"

She hesitated. "If you're really interested . . . but not

now, Rob. Something has come up in connection with the biography."

"I suspected as much. Your half of the canary seems to be sticking in your throat. Does the something that's come up have to do with those papers in your lap?"

He was looking at her warmly, and Nickie suddenly brightened. Reluctantly or not, Rob had committed himself to the book; that had been the big hurdle, and why should there be any further obstacles? "This is an outline for the remainder of the biography," she explained. "But there's one problem."

"Only one?" he teased. "Let me look at the outline and see if I can guess the problem."

Silently, Nickie handed him the outline and watched warily as he perused it.

"So far, so good," he commented when he had finished. "But the problem is obvious. The page on my love life is blank except for the chapter heading."

His matter-of-fact reaction was an immense relief to her, and she smiled. But she quickly sobered again. "We haven't discussed this very personal subject at all, Rob."

"No"—his eyes were mischievous—"but you have some firsthand experience of my lovemaking, and I'd be happy to give you more."

"Rob, be serious. Can you make some time tomorrow morning to talk to me about the women in your life?"

"You realize I'm not going to give you any juicy exposé material," he warned, but he still seemed relaxed.

"Yes. Just as I know you trust me to handle the subject with all due delicacy."

"I suppose I do. Still . . ." He hesitated.

"What is it, Rob?"

"Nickie, it's not that I think I'm entitled to a quid pro quo, or anything like that. But I would feel more comfortable telling you about the women in my life if I knew something about the men in yours."

"Oh!" Nickie was taken aback, but she realized she

didn't feel upset by the request, as she would have a few weeks ago. For one thing, the wounds her experience with Gregory had left were somehow not quite so raw now. And also, she suddenly realized, there would be an advantage in talking to Rob about Gregory. It would make it much easier for Rob to reveal whatever factors had made the subject of Joan Weldon so difficult for him if Nickie first discussed her own painful romance.

She took a deep breath. "There's only been one man in my life, Rob. I mean, only one serious love affair. His name was...is...Gregory Thompson."

Rob's eyes narrowed. "Gregory Thompson? The best-selling novelist? I haven't read his book, but I've seen all the newspaper publicity about it, especially now that they're making it into a movie."

"Yes. I'm talking about that Gregory Thompson." The fact that Gregory was well known somehow made it more awkward for her to talk about him, and Nickie wondered if similar feelings didn't account for Rob's reticence about Joan.

"I see. How did you meet him, Nickie? At a writers' conference?" Rob prodded gently.

"Not exactly. He taught a course I took at the New School," she said slowly. "He was so constructive in his comments on my papers that I showed him other things I was starting to write. It was all so proper at first." She smiled ruefully. "I'd stay after class and we'd go out for coffee or a glass of wine afterward. I was flattered and very infatuated with him. He was twenty years older, experienced, cosmopolitan, a successful editor and writer."

"And when the course was over?" Rob probed thoughtfully, draping a sympathetic arm around her shoulder.

"We celebrated with an 'intimate dinner' in the loft. We...made love. I began spending more and more time there, and he gave me a key so I could let myself in."

She shook her head. "When he asked me to do some typing for him or look at papers he was grading for another course, I was flattered. Besides, he had helped me with an article I had sold. It seemed a fair return," she explained.

"Not to me, it doesn't!" Rob said firmly.

Nickie smiled again, nestling in the comforting circle of his arm. "When the lease on my apartment was up, the landlord was going to raise the rent, and Gregory suggested that I move in with him. He had plenty of room. It seemed like a good idea since I was spending so much time there anyway, and by then I thought I was really in love with him. When he suggested I quit my job to help with his novel, how could I say no?" she asked rhetorically.

"I bet that was in bed," Rob said grimly.

Nickie nodded. "So I did the research, the interviews, the typing. It seemed so exciting at the time, especially when Louise and Gregory's editor raved about the novel and started talking movie rights and serialization. But when Gregory became famous overnight, his old friends weren't good enough for him, and neither was the loft. I guess I wasn't good enough, either. But when he moved out, I was glad, because I could stay on there and—"

"Damn it, Nickie, couldn't you see that he was using you, exploiting your 'hero worship'? I'll bet he never paid you a cent for all the work you did because you were staying there for free and supposed to be grateful that he took you to bed now and then," Rob exploded.

Nickie stared at him, taken aback by his vehemence and the anger that darkened his eyes. "I know that now. I must have guessed it at the time, but I couldn't believe, didn't want to believe, that he didn't love me," she admitted. "I was stupid."

"You weren't stupid." Rob's lips brushed her forehead and cheek. "You said it yourself—you thought you were in love. You were infatuated, and he took advantage of you. I may have my faults, but I would never cold-bloodedly use a woman like that." He paused. "You haven't told me everything, have you? Isn't it true that a lot of the novel was *your* work, not Gregory's?"

"Well, not a *lot,*" Nickie protested.

"You're being modest. Louise made a vague reference to your getting a raw deal on a previous collaboration. Now I see what she meant. I can also see that your own novel must be very important to you." He cupped her chin in one hand and tilted her face to his. "I think you should finish the novel. Use the advance from the biography for that, and if you need more—well, I'm always looking for sound investments. We can write the biography when you're finished. To hell with Burton Shields." He grinned. "I've never cared what people thought of me before—and I still don't."

Nickie stared at him, unable to speak. He was so generous, she was moved nearly to tears; but she shook her head at the tempting offer.

"Why not, Nickie?" Rob's eyes sparkled. "Louise has faith in you, and as far as I'm concerned, what you did in those first two chapters..." He shrugged, as if embarrassed. "Your novel should come first," he urged, his arm tightening around her.

"No," Nickie murmured, her cheek on his shoulder. What an honorable man Rob was for thinking of her before his own interest. Considering the circumstances and Shields's reputation, she could not imagine another man postponing a book that was so important to him.

"Are you sure?" Rob's mouth brushed against her cheek, his lips kissing the softness, moving to her eyes, the tip of her nose.

Nickie raised her head eagerly as his mouth sought hers, crushing it, his tongue teasing her lips and seeking out her tongue. A glorious spark flickered deep inside her, then burst into a flame that spread from her loins to her fingertips.

"Are you sure?" Rob whispered again, his lips nibbling the pink shell of her ear and his mischievous tongue teasing it.

Nickie felt a quivering sensation at her core. "I'm sure," she repeated. "The biography's important, too, Rob."

He sighed. "The thing is, I wouldn't want anyone but you to do the biography now. I trust you, Nickie. I . . . care for you. But I feel selfish, depriving you of time for your own work. You've had one selfish man in your life already."

"Oh, Rob," she said, "I don't think you're being selfish at all. Just the opposite. And I trust you and . . . care for you, too."

"Do you?" His breath was warm in her ear. "You know how I want you, Nickie," he said urgently. "Will you trust me to love you? I can imagine that Thompson was as selfish sexually as he was in other ways, but it doesn't have to be like that, darling. Let me show you, let me give to you . . ."

"Rob, the book . . ."

"I know, but the book is going well now. It will go even better without all this tension between us." His hand lightly stroked her breast, and the nipple rose with longing to his touch.

Nickie sighed, finally admitting to herself that she loved Rob—wasn't merely infatuated as she had been with Gregory, but loved him with all her being. Indeed, that was the real reason she'd been able to talk to Rob about Gregory—because she'd felt so close to him, had wanted to share everything with him, even her pain. And now, how could she refuse this final sharing, this ultimate closeness, when she craved it as much as he did?

"Oh, Rob, I do want you," she breathed.

"Nickie, my sweet, sweet love. I'll be good to you, darling, so good." And with infinite tenderness, he cradled her in his arms, then picked her up and gently lowered her to the thick Persian carpet. His strong hands fondled her breasts with tantalizing slowness, while his soft lips nibbled at hers. Then his tongue became a sweet plunderer, sucking the honeyed treasure of her mouth as his hand slipped beneath her T-shirt and deftly unhooked her bra. The touch of his fingers on her breasts was a pleasuring torment, causing her whole being to ache for him.

"You feel so soft, so glorious," he murmured. "Let me look at you." Lovingly, he removed her shirt and bra, and gazed reverently at her high, firm breasts. Then he took one taut nipple in his mouth, teasing it with his tongue, as his questing hands moved down over her flat stomach and unzipped her jeans. He slid them over her hips, off her legs, and her lacy bikini panties with them. His fingers lightly stroked the down-covered mound at the parting of her thighs, then gently probed deeper, deeper, sending pinpricks of need and desire to her very core.

"I want to see you, touch you, too," she said hoarsely, reaching for his shirt buttons and undoing them with trembling fingers. She drew the fabric off his powerful shoulders and tossed the shirt aside, then unfastened his belt buckle. She peeled away his pants and gasped at this first sight of him completely naked. He was so huge, so magnificent, so uncompromisingly male. She touched him shyly at first, then grew bolder and let her hand wander down his taut abdomen to stroke the silky shaft of his desire till he groaned with passion.

Against their naked skin the soft velvet of the rug felt like the grass of an enchanted garden. In wonder and excitement, they explored each other's bodies for the first time, discovering one another's most erogenous places and climbing toward the heights of ecstasy with mounting urgency.

As they pressed ever closer together, their legs becoming entwined, Nickie could feel Rob's swollen manhood straining against her thigh. His fingers caressed her buttocks and light, rippling motions.

"Rob, Rob, please. I want you so much," she moaned.

"Not yet, Nickie, but soon," he said huskily, as his fingers once more found the center of her need and sent fiery shockwaves to her innermost being. "You're so silky, so wet," he said, breathing heavily.

Her body was moving wildly at his touch. "You're torturing me," she gasped. "Oh, please, Rob."

"Yes, my love, now," he reassured her. He lifted his body over hers and paused, throbbing, powerful, his eyes locked on hers, piercing to her very soul. She was completely open and vulnerable to him, and for a brief instant she yearned to hide her naked longing. But his eyes held hers in an implacable bond. And in another instant reassurance poured into her, as if he had recognized her need and filled it with a power of his own. She met his gaze boldly, unashamed of her desire, reveling in her power to hold and transfix him, just as he held her passionately enthralled. And then he entered her, ever so slowly, as if afraid of hurting her, and she was swept away.

His first thrusts were gentle, tentative. But as she arched in welcome and he felt how pliant, how ready for him she was, he gradually quickened the pace of their lovemaking. A crescendo of sensation was building and building inside her, consuming her.

They were moving as one being, each lost in the other. Nickie felt irrevocably joined to Rob, more complete than she had ever felt before. What bliss it was to be fiercely united to him, merged in his being and he in hers.

"Nickie, my own Nickie," he murmured, raining feather-light kisses on her hair, her cheek, her throat. Then his lips claimed hers in an ardent kiss as the crescendo peaked in waves of exquisite pleasure that went on and on.

Slowly, reluctantly, they came back to an awareness of themselves. Their bodies still joined, their two hearts beat as one. Rob eased himself away from Nickie and drew her against his matted chest, kissing the top of her head as he tenderly fondled her breasts.

"It was so beautiful," she told him in an awed whisper, stroking the soft hair on his thigh.

"It will always be beautiful for us, Nickie," he said hoarsely. "I won't ask you to move in again, now that you've told me about Gregory, but once the book's finished and I can tell the world how I feel about you, I—"

She stopped him with a kiss, afraid that promises uttered in the first flush of ecstasy might later be regretted...retracted. Yet when the kiss ended, he said reproachfully, "You don't trust me yet—not really. But you will, I swear it."

"Please, Rob, don't say any more. It's all so new, so fragile. Let's just take things one step at a time...see where we're going."

He sighed. "I've known where we were going from the moment I looked into those enchanting green eyes of yours. But all right, I understand. We won't talk about the future. But at least tell me you'll stay here tonight. It's Burns's night off, so we'll be alone."

"Rob, I can't. I have only these clothes. Tomorrow morning...No, it's impossible. In fact, I really ought to be going now."

"No! At least stay for dinner...and for a while afterward. Then I'll drive you home myself, if you still insist on going."

"You know I want to spend the night with you," she told him, "but I can't."

"You will come back tomorrow?"

"To work," she said firmly. "We're going to talk in the morning, remember? I still have to fill in that blank page about...the women in your life."

"You're the only woman in my life right now," he

told her. "I don't even want to think about others. But all right, I'll make time in the morning for that interview."

"If you've got a busy schedule, perhaps we should do it tonight," she suggested. "I promised Louise I'd get the outline done right away."

"Tomorrow's time enough. I'll rearrange my schedule. Not another word about it now." He laid her gently on the carpet again, and covered her body with his. "Tonight," he said huskily, "there's no one in the universe except you and me."

Chapter Eight

THE NEXT MORNING, Nickie followed Burns to Rob's library with mixed emotions. Now that she and Rob were lovers, it would be difficult to revert to her role as his biographer, to compartmentalize their relationship that way. One look at Rob's face told her that he was struggling with the same problem. He greeted her impersonally in front of Burns, busying himself with pouring coffee until the houseman had left.

As soon as they were alone, he drew her into his arms. "I hardly slept last night," he said. "I kept thinking about you, wishing you had stayed with me."

It took a tremendous effort to extricate herself from his embrace. "Oh, Rob, I felt the same way, but we have to remember I'm here today to interview you for the book."

"I know, I know." He ran a hand through his chestnut hair in a gesture of frustration and moved restlessly away. "I'm not trying to sabotage the biography, but I wish it didn't have to be this way. I'd rather tell you about my love life the way lovers share their pasts, the way you shared yours with me. Instead, you're going to be sitting here taking notes, writing down everything for the whole damn world to read." He sent her an agonized look, but there was nothing she could say. She, too, dreaded the job before them, but they had no choice. "Oh, well, let's get it over with." He strode back to his desk and gave her a suddenly cheeky grin. "You'd better take that chair on the other side of the desk. Otherwise, I refuse to be responsible for what happens."

Unable to keep from grinning in response, she seated herself in the leather chair he had indicated and took a sip of coffee. If only he didn't look so devilishly handsome in his casual yet elegant blue sports jacket and creased cream-colored slacks. She herself had felt an uncharacteristic hesitation in selecting an outfit today, finally choosing a pencil-slim white cotton skirt and a silky short-sleeved mauve blouse. She had told herself it was a cool outfit for a hot day, but had she unconsciously picked the skirt because it displayed the long, slim legs that Rob had several times admired, and the blouse because it clung to her breasts in an alluringly feminine manner? She sighed. Rob wasn't the only one sending out mixed messages this morning.

He was looking at her expectantly, and Nickie quickly reached into her purse for notebook and pen. "Perhaps it will be easier if we start with some of your . . . less intense relationships," she suggested, feeling suddenly shy. "I mean, why don't we begin with your general reputation as a man-about-town. Your name has been linked with quite a number of socialites and actresses . . ."

He chuckled and sent her a teasing glance. "Actually, I'm hardly the ladykiller the press makes me out to be. Many of my dates with movie stars or starlets are arranged by studio publicity departments, and I don't even meet the woman until I show up at her door to escort her to her latest preview or whatever."

"Why would you want to go out with a woman you don't know?" Nickie asked.

He shot her a devilish grin. "Maybe because I want to know her; obviously, the film world is full of attractive and interesting women. Or simply in the hopes of an enjoyable evening. Every date can't be the prelude to a heavy love affair, after all. I'll go out with an actress a few times, and then maybe we don't see each other for a while, what with my business trips, her going off to distant filming locations, yet there are no hurt feelings on either side."

Nickie kept her head bent over her notebook so Rob would see no sign of her inner turmoil. He seemed to be saying he preferred women who didn't expect or want commitments, and what did that bode for their relationship once the book was finished?

"Of course, not all the actresses I've dated have been Hollywood types," Rob continued. "With my business based in New York, I tend to meet a number of Broadway actresses as well."

"Yes, over the years you seem to have had an on-again, off-again romance with Anita Fullbright," Nickie remarked.

Rob's laughter was free of embarrassment. "That's right—when Anita is between husbands. Shall I tell you about her? She'd love the publicity. I ran into her recently and she was complaining about being passed over for several leading roles in favor of younger women."

"She was pretty young herself when you two first started seeing each other, wasn't she?"

"So she was." Rob paused to drink his coffee. "Let's see, I met Anita at a party shortly after I bought out Bach. She was an ingenue in a play that had flopped. We were an 'item,' as the columnists say," he went on, a note of amusement in his voice as he told her how Anita had grabbed the headlines with him until she went into another play, at which time she had started seeing the leading man, who became her first husband.

"That marriage lasted only a few months," Nickie recalled. "And then you and Anita picked up where you had left off?"

"Her husband had a roving eye, and that was quite a blow to Anita's pride," he said. "She told me quite honestly that she wanted it to seem as if she had left him for an old flame. We managed to get ourselves photographed together at all the 'in' nightspots, and Anita even arranged a torrid sidewalk embrace that made the front cover of several movie magazines. After her second husband—also a philanderer—it was the same thing. Her third husband, the producer, died, and Anita was genuinely broken up about that one. In fact, she suffered a nervous breakdown. By that time, we were old friends and I started dating her again, more to get her back into the social swing than anything else."

"You make it sound as if there was more smoke than fire," Nickie commented, "but wasn't there some kind of feud between Anita and another actress over you?"

Rob nodded. "Gilda Ramey was the other actress, but the feud really had nothing to do with me. Still, there was that incident at Regine's . . ."

Nickie noticed that Rob had become increasingly enthusiastic in his reminiscences. He was actually enjoying her probing! The colorful anecdotes he related would certainly add spice to the book, but she couldn't help feeling a twinge of jealousy as he described episode after episode with one actress or another. Sometimes he would forget a name and refer merely to "that stunning redhead" or "a very voluptuous brunette," and Nickie wondered if someday he would recall "the black-haired writer with the sensational legs" in the same casual fashion. Suddenly, she felt she'd been a fool to think she meant anything special to him.

"Well, I think that covers the actresses—what do you say?" he interrupted her thoughts.

"Yes, I think we can move on to the socialites," she agreed with a hint of irony.

Failing to pick up on her growing moodiness, he shrugged. "A number of prominent bachelors, myself included, are asked from time to time to round out some society matron's guest list. Then there are the charity galas, the fund-raising dinners for the arts and the public library, opening night at the opera..."

"And the debutante balls," Nickie supplied.

"Ah yes, the debutante balls." Rob grimaced. "Fortunately, I'm now considered a bit too 'mature' to be invited to many of those, but in my younger days I was constantly being called upon to help fill out the roster. I even became rather infatuated with one young lady, but her mother soon let me know my blood wasn't blue enough—before I'd had a chance to fall seriously in love."

"But you have been...seriously in love?" Nickie asked with a slight tremor in her voice.

His eyes were somber as they met her inquiring gaze. "Yes. The first time it was really more puppy love, although I had a different perspective then. I was a sophomore at Princeton when I met Betty, a Vassar student, at a mixer. From then on, I spent my weekends commuting back and forth between Princeton and Poughkeepsie, and Betty always came to the football and baseball games to see me play and celebrate the victories afterward."

"What was it about Betty that made her so special?"

He considered. "She was pretty, of course, but I guess it was mainly her sense of humor. I was so intense, and she made me laugh, taught me how to relax."

"But...?"

He gave a rueful smile. "I guess you can have too much of a good thing. That summer, Betty went to Europe with her family, so I didn't see her. We wrote, but sporadically, and when we did finally get together again in the fall"—he shrugged—"somehow the magic was gone. I guess I'd started looking for her serious side, and there didn't seem to be one. I got tired of all the jokes."

"I see. So that was your first love. And then?"

"And then nothing—I mean nothing I thought of as love—until about five years ago. That's when I met . . . I'll call her Jessie. She's married to someone else now and might not appreciate my using her real name. Anyway, she was the personnel director of a firm out in White Plains that I was doing business with at the time. One day, I saw her coming out of a vice-president's office, and followed her down the corridor until I could corner her at a water fountain and introduce myself—completely forgetting about my own appointment with the vice-president." He looked at Nickie with a tentative smile. "As you know, when I want something, I go after it."

Nickie tried to keep her features impassive. "And you wanted Jessie," she said.

"Yes, I wanted Jessie. She had a quality, a sort of jaunty air, I don't know what to call it. I just took one look at her and said to myself, *That's the one*. It was almost spooky. And when I got to know her, she was just what I'd imagined—so natural, totally unaffected, very different from the women I'd been dating in Manhattan. Well, we clicked, began to see a lot of each other, and after a few months started to talk about getting married."

"You were engaged?" Nickie asked the question calmly, but inside she felt as if she were slowly dying. How could she hope to compete with all these women—past, present, and future? How could she hope to win Rob's love?

"We weren't officially engaged," he went on. "In fact, the press never got onto this one; we rarely went out in

Manhattan. I usually drove up to White Plains for our dates."

"Was that your choice or hers?"

"It was a mutual decision. Jessie had an outgoing personality, but she considered her private life very private; she told me that right off. I was somewhat tired of the limelight myself, and I have to admit it was reassuring to know that here was one woman who really cared about me for myself, wasn't using me to get publicity or anything like that. It was obvious, too, that Jessie wasn't after my money. I used to tease her about being a 'cheap date' because, more often than not, we'd spend our evenings visiting with one or another of her relatives. She came from a large family and was very close to several married sisters."

"Was that a problem for you?"

He looked surprised. "Oh, no, I liked them a lot—the sisters, their husbands, Jessie's parents. They were like the family I never had." He smiled wistfully.

"Did you get tired of Jessie?"

He shook his head. "No, that wasn't it, either. She got fed up with my peripatetic lifestyle. At first, when I had to go on business trips, she was a good sport about it. Then she began to complain. I wanted to work things out, but I was in the midst of building an empire, and I had to travel. I got Jessie to take some vacation time from her job and come to Paris with me on one of my trips, but it turned out to be a fiasco. I had meetings, got tied up, came back to the hotel late . . . That was it as far as Jessie was concerned. She told me flatly she couldn't marry a man who didn't have time for her."

"Couldn't you have made more time?"

"I could never have been the kind of husband she wanted, one who'd be home for dinner every night by six-thirty at the latest. She wanted someone like her father, who had his own business at home and had always been there for her when she was growing up. She wanted children right away, too, and kept saying she didn't want to raise them all by herself. I understood her point of view, could even admit the virtues of it, but I simply couldn't be what she wanted."

"So she married someone else. But how did you know that?"

"Oh, I saw the announcement of the wedding in *The New York Times*. She married a free-lance artist—a successful one—and I imagine she's happy with him. I wish them well."

"You're not still in love with her, even a little?"

"No. Someone else came into my life . . ."

Joan Weldon. Nickie didn't say the name aloud, but only, "I can guess who that was."

He quirked an eyebrow at her. "I should hope so. But of course you're not going to write about us in the biography."

"Us? Oh, you were talking about me." Nickie was both pleased and disconcerted. "No, of course I'm not going to write about us." After hearing about all the women in his life, she couldn't help wondering with some confusion how she fit into the long list. Their affair would probably be so brief that it wouldn't even rate a casual mention in the biography—if someone else were writing it.

"So, that's it then," Rob said. "Time for a nice long lunch . . . starting with dessert." He rose and came meaningfully toward her, taking the notebook and pen from her hand and placing them on the desk. But as he drew her to her feet and circled her waist with his masterful arms, she knew she couldn't kiss him, make love to him, when she felt so uncertain of his feelings for her—and his ultimate intentions.

"Rob . . ."

"Come on, Nickie, the interview is over. Don't I even get a kiss, or two, or three?"

He cupped her chin and tilted it upward, but she broke away, suddenly remembering the one woman he hadn't mentioned. "Rob, the interview's *not* over. What about Joan Weldon?"

His face lost all traces of tenderness, and his features hardened into granite. "There's to be no mention of Joan Weldon in this book. I thought Louise understood that. I certainly made it plain to those two other writers she sent to interview me."

"But, Rob—"

"I said no! Joan is dead, her parents have suffered enough, and I won't be a party to anything that would cause further pain."

"But Shields—"

"I don't care what Shields says. He has no facts, only gossip and innuendo, and I won't dignify his mud by replying to it."

Nickie made a gesture of protest, some of her anger at Rob—however unreasonable—for having so many women in his past spilling over into her anger at him for refusing to discuss Joan Weldon. "I thought the whole point of this authorized biography was to counteract Shields's smear campaign against you."

"As far as my business dealings go, yes. But he can say what he likes about my private life, and damn anyone who believes him. My conscience is clear."

"Then why don't you clear up the mystery once and for all? If you have nothing to fear in regard to the Joan Weldon story, why won't you talk about her?"

"Because there's nothing to talk about. Nothing that belongs in my biography anyway."

"You're not denying that you dated her?" Nickie asked incredulously.

"No, of course I don't deny that. But every woman I ever dated isn't being mentioned in the book."

"Every woman you ever dated didn't die under mysterious circumstances. Joan Weldon took an overdose of drugs. You were called to the inquest..."

"What are you getting at, Nickie? Do you think I murdered her?"

"It's not a question of what I think."

"Isn't it? It seems to me we're back to the issue of trust. If you trusted me, my telling you I had nothing to do with Joan Weldon's death would be enough."

"Rob, don't bring our personal relationship into this. I resent—"

"You resent? That's rich. Tell me, Nickie"—his voice was hard—"have you been deliberately softening me up in order to get me to tell you about Joan Weldon?"

She stared at him, shocked. "What are you talking about?"

"It would really be quite a feather in your cap to get me to talk about Joan, wouldn't it? You knew I'd always refused to discuss the subject with anyone else, but maybe you thought that if we were sleeping together..."

"Oh, you're despicable!" Before she realized it, her hand had moved of its own accord, and she felt the impact as it connected squarely with Rob's cheek. For a moment, they looked at each other in stunned silence, then Rob dazedly stroked the red mark on his face where Nickie had slapped him.

Nickie was appalled. "I—I'm sorry," she said finally. "I've never done anything like that before in my life. But what you said..." She swallowed the lump in her throat and blinked against the tears that had risen to her eyes.

"What I said *was* despicable—since it wasn't true." His arms were around her instantly, his strong yet gentle fingers patting her back in soothing motions. "Nickie, darling, forgive me. I had to be sure that you truly cared about me, that it wasn't all for the book. I'm sure we can work this out."

"I don't see how," she murmured. "We should never—"

"Hush! I won't let you say it. Now, we've compromised before; let's see if we can't come up with a compromise on this." He led her to the sofa and drew her down beside him. "All right, you can mention Joan in the book. Include her name with the other socially prominent women I've dated, and you can even quote me as saying her early death was a tragedy."

"But, Rob—"

"Nickie, just write what I told you."

"But everyone knows what you told me. It will seem as if we're glossing over the scandal."

"There was nothing scandalous about my relationship with Joan!"

"Then why all this secrecy?"

He paced the room in exasperation. "We're going around in circles, damn it. Look, Nickie, you know all *my* secrets. As far as I'm concerned, Joan's are buried with her. This book's publication shouldn't depend on the rehashing of some old gossip. Smalley's a man of integrity, and if he likes what you've written so far, there will be a book."

"I'm not sure he'll see it quite that way, Rob. Louise—"

"Well, call Louise then and talk to her about it. I say we should leave the decision to Smalley. Look, I'm going out to the terrace. After you've spoken to Louise, why don't you join me there for lunch."

"She may be out to lunch herself, but I will call."

Louise answered the phone herself. "Finally!" she said. "I've been trying to get through to you all morning, but Starr's secretary said her orders were to hold all calls. I even had a sandwich sent in on the off-chance you'd call during lunch. I've got great news, Nickie."

"Smalley's read the chapters? He likes them?" Nickie could hardly contain her excitement.

"He loves them! I've never heard Richard Smalley so enthusiastic about a new writer. Now, as I anticipated, he'd like to see an outline, and also another chapter, to bring the page total to a hundred. I know it's asking a lot, Nickie, but could you have the additional chapter and the outline for me tomorrow? Smalley wants to see us Friday morning, so I'd like to get him the outline and extra chapter by five tomorrow. He said he'd take them home with him to look at."

"I can have the Bach chapter for you then, and the outline," Nickie promised. "But listen, Louise, I'd better tell you about my interview with Rob this morning." Briefly, Nickie summarized all that Rob had told her—and all he had refused to tell her. She omitted any mention of her own involvement with Rob, or the emotional aspects of their quarrel.

"Well, of course I'd be happier if you'd gotten the whole story out of him," Louise commented, "but the situation doesn't sound exactly hopeless. Perhaps we can just persuade him to say in the book that he had nothing to do with Joan's death. Anyway, I think Rob's right about leaving the decision to Smalley. Perhaps the new information that Rob was once on the verge of marriage, and the true story of the Bach takeover . . . well, we'll just have to see. But you're sure you can have the outline and the Bach chapter for me tomorrow?"

"I'll have them," Nickie assured her. "Even if I have to stay up all night!"

Chapter Nine

WHEN SHE WENT up to the terrace, Nickie found Rob poring over a pile of phone messages on his desk.

"Business, business, business," he said ruefully, pushing aside the pink message slips as Nickie joined him at the wrought-iron table.

She glanced at the top slip, and a familiar name caught her eye. "You're doing business with Anita Fullbright?" she teased.

He gave a sheepish grin. "I forgot about that one. I have no idea what Anita wants."

"Maybe she's between husbands again," Nickie suggested dryly, telling herself she had no reason to feel jealous, since Rob had told her all about his long friendship with the actress and was clearly not in love with her. Yet Nickie suspected that the relationship was not completely platonic.

As if reading her thoughts, Rob said, "Well, if she is, I'll just have to tell her I'm otherwise occupied, won't

I? Oh, by the way, Joyce said there were some calls for you, but they were all from Louise."

"I know. I just spoke to her. Smalley wants to meet with us Friday morning."

"Oh?" Rob frowned. "Look, can't you and Louise handle it without me? I'm in the midst of some negotiations over an oil operation in the North Sea. I'm swamped with work, and taking time out for the interview this morning didn't help any."

"I know you're busy, Rob, but Smalley may have questions that only you can answer. It probably won't take more than an hour."

"Oh, all right. I'll check my schedule with Joyce. Good afternoon, Burns," he greeted the houseman, who was wheeling a food trolley out onto the terrace. "Is that your famous lobster Bahamas-style I see?"

The houseman smiled. "Yes, Mr. Starr." He turned to Nickie. "In this humid weather, Mr. Starr often isn't too hungry, but he always likes my lobster salad. I make it with fresh coconut, apple, walnuts, and my own home-made mayonnaise."

"Sounds delicious," Nickie said sincerely.

"I think you'll like it, Miss Monroe." Burns set out two plates for them, on which he arranged the lobster salad attractively. Then he placed a wineglass at each table setting, and took a bottle of Riesling from the ice bucket and opened it. First he poured for Rob, who tasted the wine and nodded, and then he filled Nickie's glass as well.

"Just leave the ice bucket here on the trolley, Burns," Rob instructed.

"Yes, sir," the houseman said, and departed with a slight bow in Nickie's direction.

"He really is perfect," Nickie said, wondering if she should work a Burns-like character into her novel.

"Hmm? Oh, yes, Burns is a gem. Taste your wine,

Nickie," Rob urged. "It's an excellent vintage."

She sighed. "Well, I'll taste it, but not much more. "I'm afraid it will go to my head, and I have a hard day's work before me." She sipped the wine, remarking on its excellence, and then explained that she had promised Louise she would have the outline and Bach chapter ready the next day. "I have most of the information for the Bach chapter already," she said, "but I do need to ask you a few questions. Since you're going to be tied up this afternoon, maybe we'd better take care of it now." She reached into her pocketbook for a memo pad.

"You're unbelievable," Rob said, shaking his head. "Do you always carry a spare notebook with you—just in case?"

Nickie laughed. "Actually, I do. You see, I never know when I'll come across something I might want to use in my writing. On the subway, in line at the supermarket, I sometimes get ideas, and this way I can jot down my thoughts so I can refer to them when I actually sit down to write."

Rob chuckled. "Shakespeare said all the world's a stage, but in your case it seems to be a book."

"Or series of books," Nickie agreed. "Anyway, to get back to *this* book, let me ask you those questions."

She had just finished writing his answer to the last question when Burns reappeared with a tray bearing two dishes of pink sherbet with a fresh strawberry on top of each.

"The lobster salad was out of this world," Nickie told him.

"I'm glad you liked it, Miss Monroe. And for dessert, I thought strawberry sherbet might be refreshing." The houseman set a dish before each of them, then stacked their plates and wineglasses on the trolley and wheeled it away.

"Strawberries are becoming a regular thing with us,"

Rob remarked. "I'm beginning to think of you as my strawberry lady."

Nickie grinned. "I suspect you gave Burns specific instructions about dessert."

"Who, me?" Rob's air of exaggerated innocence was endearing. "Now why would I do that?"

"So you could do this—only it's my turn." She took the strawberry from atop her sherbet and popped it into his mouth, caressing his full lower lip with her forefinger. He grasped her wrist lightly and licked each of her fingers in turn, sending a delicious shiver up her spine.

"My favorite dessert," he said archly. "Strawberries are a poor second."

Even on the shady terrace, the midday sun was bearing down on them, and they ate their sherbet quickly, before it could melt.

"I wish we could linger awhile, but we've both got work to do," Rob said, pushing back his chair. "Perhaps tonight we can go out for dinner together?"

"I'd like that," Nickie agreed, glowing inside at the thought of their first real date.

Some time later, she had finished the rough draft of the Bach chapter and was thinking of the evening ahead with joyful anticipation when Rob came through the connecting door from the library.

"I'm afraid we'll have to postpone our dinner," he said apologetically. "Something's come up in connection with that oil deal I mentioned earlier."

"I understand," she said, trying to keep her disappointment from showing. "Oh, well, that will give me some more time to polish the outline and the Bach chapter at home tonight. Do you have a moment to check the new chapter for accuracy?"

She gave him the typescript, and he glanced through it quickly. "Damn it, Nickie, you might have told me you were going to get Bach's version of the story, although since you've gotten the man to hang himself, I suppose I have no grounds for complaint. You really are incorrigible, though." He put aside the papers and drew her into his arms.

"I warned you that I have to do things my own way," Nickie reminded him, snuggling against his broad chest.

"So you did. And you have such a cute, appealing way of doing so many things," he said suggestively. He tilted her head up to his, but Nickie was disappointed by the perfunctory kiss he gave her.

"No time," he said regretfully. "If I let you have your way with me now, I'm liable to let that oil deal go to the four winds. You'll be here in the morning?"

"Sure," she said, busying herself with the papers to hide her vexation.

She had just let herself into the loft an hour and a half later when her phone began to ring. She made a quick dive for the instrument, hoping that during her long subway ride something had happened to change Rob's plans and that he was calling to say he could keep their dinner date after all. But it was Jack Naughton calling.

"Oh, hello, Jack," she said, suddenly remembering their talk about getting together for a drink. "How are you?"

"I'm fine, Nickie, but I really didn't call to exchange amenities. Are you still interested in hearing what I have to tell you about your . . . friend, Rob Starr?"

"Yes," Nickie said slowly, wondering at her lack of enthusiasm, which she knew was due to more than Jack's rudeness. Was it that she now had so much evidence in Rob's favor that she could no longer believe Jack knew anything really damaging about him? Or, in her heart of hearts, was she afraid she might hear something that would give her cause to doubt the man she loved?

"Well, I'm going to be in your neck of the woods— the West Village—tomorrow morning. Perhaps we could have lunch together and talk then?"

"Lunch?" Nickie echoed, thinking that it would hardly be worthwhile to make the long subway ride up to Rob's, come back to the Village for lunch, and then return uptown. "Could we make it later in the afternoon, Jack? For drinks, as we originally discussed?"

"That wouldn't be convenient for me," he said curtly. "If you can't make it tomorrow, perhaps next week..."

Nickie hesitated, toying with the telephone cord. "Jack, can you give me some idea of what this is all about?"

"Well, I really don't want to go into it over the phone," he said, "but it has to do with Joan Weldon—and her suicide."

Nickie felt the blood drain from her face. Joan was the one subject about which Rob continued to be evasive. She had believed him when he said he'd nothing to do with the heiress's death, but Jack's tone implied otherwise. Nickie suddenly decided she had better see Jack; she was uneasy, and not only because of the biography.

"Okay, we'll make it lunch tomorrow," she told him. "Where do you want to meet?"

"How about the White Horse Inn? Seeing as you're a writer and the place has literary associations with Dylan Thomas and Brendan Behan. They also make the best cheeseburgers in town. And they do their main business at night, so we won't have to worry about privacy."

"The White Horse is fine. What time shall we meet?"

"How's twelve-thirty?"

"Twelve-thirty is fine."

"Good, then I'll see you tomorrow." He hung up abruptly, and Nickie remembered Rob's characterization of Jack as boorish. But had Rob only been trying to discredit Jack because he knew the younger man could discredit him?

She would put the whole subject out of her mind until she heard what Jack had to say, Nickie decided. With trembling fingers she dialed Rob's number; she would have to tell him that she'd be working at home tomorrow. With any luck, he would already have left for the evening and she wouldn't have to go into any explanations. Much to her relief, Burns informed her that Rob was not at home.

"Shall I tell him to call you when he gets in, Miss Monroe?" the houseman inquired. "It may be very late, but if it's a matter of importance . . ."

"No, no, I simply wanted to let him know that I won't be coming up in the morning after all, Burns," she explained. "Tell him I'll call him in the afternoon."

"Yes, Miss Monroe. I'll see that he gets the message."

After telling Burns good-bye, Nickie went into the kitchen to fix herself a sandwich. The bread was going stale, and she couldn't help making an unfavorable comparison between her own mixture of tuna and mayo and Burns's exquisite lobster salad.

"Nickie Monroe," she lectured herself, "you're getting spoiled." Yet she knew there was more to her lack of appetite than that. Though she tried not to speculate on what Jack might say, her stomach was aswarm with butterflies, leaving no room for food.

Nickie found herself unable to concentrate on her writing that evening and went to bed early. She awoke the next morning feeling more refreshed, and had finished her editing and retyping by noon. Although it would only take her a few minutes to walk to the White Horse, she decided to be on her way; it was so hot in the loft, and she could always delay her arrival at the tavern by window-shopping along the way.

Out on the street, Nickie noticed that a cool breeze had sprung up, clearing the air of engine exhaust and the usual city smells. Savoring the freshness, she walked slowly east to Hudson Street and then uptown, stopping now and then to look in the windows of the antique shops that lined both sides of the street. Most were filled with what looked to Nickie like secondhand furniture badly in need of repair and bric-a-brac that only seemed to be antique in condition. At the White Horse, she went inside. Just a few customers were in the landmark tavern with its dark interior, uneven wooden floors, big old-fashioned bar, and fragile stools, and she decided to sit outside at one of the picnic tables in the outdoor café.

Before she had time to order, Jack arrived.

Nickie smiled at him. "Do you want to sit outside or inside?"

"The inside may have more atmosphere, but let's sit here." Jack took a seat on the bench opposite Nickie and mopped his face with a damp handkerchief. "That breeze feels good."

"I hope this place is all right with you," Jack said as they studied the rather short menus the waitress had given them. "I would have suggested one of the fancier restaurants in the area, but I don't have unlimited time for lunch, and I knew this would be a fairly secluded place." He gestured at the empty tables around them.

"It's fine, Jack, really," Nickie assured him. "After all, we're here primarily to talk." After the waitress had taken their order for cheeseburgers and beer, she said, "There's something I ought to tell you. The work I'm doing for Rob—well, we're seeing a publisher tomorrow, so there's really no need for secrecy anymore. He's commissioned me to do an authorized biography of him—there's an unauthorized and, I gather, pretty sensationalist one being done by a writer named Burton Shields. Perhaps you've heard about it?"

Jack shook his head. "Uh-uh. I know nothing about Burton Shields or any book on Starr. But under the circumstances, it was clever of him to choose as his official biographer a naïve young woman whom he could easily charm into thinking he's Mister Wonderful."

"That's not the case," Nickie said heatedly. "I'm hardly naïve, and I've been doing my own research on Rob—

you heard me talking to your father. So far, the facts are entirely to his credit."

"So far," Jack said pointedly. "Look, I don't want to argue with you, Nickie. I'll simply tell you what I came here to say. It's not anything you'd want to use in an official biography, but should you decide to do your own unauthorized book, you're welcome to use my information any way you please. I only ask that you not mention my name. My parents go back a long way with the Weldons, not to mention Starr, and it would be awkward."

"I don't anticipate doing an unauthorized book," Nickie said steadily, although her stomach was tied up in knots of uneasiness. "However, you have my word that I won't use your name in anything I may write."

"Despite my being a lawyer, I won't ask you to put it in writing," Jack said ironically. When the waitress approached with their food, he dropped the subject, and they ate their cheeseburgers in silence.

"You were right—they make a mean cheeseburger here," Nickie told him, trying to sound lighthearted despite her growing concern over what Jack had to say about Joan Weldon.

"Nickie, believe me, I wouldn't have made this appointment if I didn't feel a sense of obligation about it. It's not easy . . ."

"Jack, it will be easier if you just level with me."

"All right, then." He took a long drink of his beer. "I don't know how much you already know about Starr and Joan," he began.

"I'm aware that they went out together pretty frequently for some months," she told him. "Rob says it wasn't a serious love affair."

Jack scowled. "Not serious as far as he was concerned, but Joan had other ideas. She was madly in love with him."

"How do you know that?" Nickie challenged him. If

it had been love, even one-sided, wouldn't Rob have told her?

"From Joan herself. You see, Nickie, along with a number of other men, I was in love with Joan. As I mentioned, my parents and hers were old friends, and we played together as children."

"You grew up together," Nickie prompted. "She was your childhood sweetheart."

"Not exactly. Joan went off to boarding school in Switzerland in early adolescence," he explained. "She later attended the Sorbonne and stayed in Paris for a few years after that. So I didn't see her again until we were both about twenty-six. I couldn't believe she was the skinny kid whose pigtails I used to pull. She was . . . well, gorgeous." He paused to drink his beer.

"I've seen pictures of her," Nickie said softly.

"They don't do her justice," Jack said fiercely. "She had the face of an angel. I was head over heels about her, but even though we were the same age, she treated me like a kid. I had taken a few years off after college, and I was just starting my senior year at Columbia Law School. Not that being older would really have helped. As I said, I wasn't the only one smitten with Joan when she came to New York."

"You saw a lot of her?"

"Inevitably"—he shrugged—"because our families were both part of the city's social scene." He made a scornful grimace. "Not that it did me much good. She was always on the arm of Rob Starr."

Nickie sipped her beer and waited for Jack to continue.

"I don't want you to think this is sour grapes," he told her. "If Starr had been as crazy about Joan as she was about him, I'd have said God bless them. But it wasn't like that. He was just fooling around with her."

"How do you know how he felt?" Nickie said, feeling a need to defend Rob.

"I won't say I got it from the horse's mouth. But I

could see that Joan wasn't very happy. Oh, she smiled
for the photographers, was gay at parties—too gay. I've
never seen anyone look as sad as Joan did sometimes
when she thought no one was watching her."

"She could have been unhappy for reasons totally
unrelated to Rob," Nickie observed, wanting to believe
this was the case.

"What else did she have to be unhappy about?" Jack
sneered. "It was obviously him. When I persisted in
asking her out after she turned me down the first time,
she came right out and told me there was no room in her
life for any other man but him. After a while, I began to
wonder when the engagement was going to be announced. I mean, the Weldons are very proper, very
concerned with appearances, and here was all this gossip-
column publicity about their only child and playboy
Thomas Robinson Starr and yet no engagement. So I
asked Joan, one time while I was dancing with her at a
party, when the wedding bells were going to ring. She
made a joke of it, but I saw that sad look on her face
again."

"Then you think Rob wouldn't marry her and that's
why she committed suicide?" Nickie probed, telling herself it was only conjecture on Jack's part. Joan had been
beautiful, wealthy, could have had her choice of other
men, after all. Nickie thought that she herself, with none
of Joan's advantages, had not even contemplated killing
herself over Gregory.

"There's more to it than that," Jack said. "I have good
reason to believe Joan was pregnant. The child had to
be Starr's—I'm quite sure she wasn't seeing anyone else.
Joan might not have committed suicide just because she
was in love with a man who wouldn't marry her, but if
she were pregnant, it would be a very different matter.
Oh, some women might get an abortion, or simply have
the child out of wedlock, but not a Weldon. I told you
they were concerned with appearances—that's probably

an understatement. They're also pillars of the Catholic Church, and Joan might have had other reasons for ruling out abortion. She was caught between a rock and a hard place: couldn't have the child, couldn't not have it. The only solution was for Starr to marry her, and he wouldn't. So she took an overdose of sleeping pills—at least she wouldn't have to face the world."

Nickie was stunned. It can't be, she told herself. It just can't be! Trying to keep her voice level, she asked, "Jack, did she tell you she was pregnant?"

He laughed sardonically. "No, she didn't tell me. A Weldon wouldn't talk about such things. If it's any comfort, I don't have what the law calls 'hard evidence.' But the circumstantial case is pretty strong, and as an attorney I can tell you that a preponderance of circumstantial evidence leads to conviction more often than not."

"And what is the circumstantial evidence?" Nickie asked dully.

"I was getting to that," he said. "Feeling the way I did about Joan, I made a point of being where she was as much as possible. That wasn't too difficult, since we were both part of the same social circle. When we were in the same room, I couldn't take my eyes off her. I began to notice that she seemed ill. She'd clutch her stomach from time to time, seem to have dizzy spells . . ."

"That could mean any number of things besides pregnancy," Nickie said eagerly, wanting to believe Jack's story was purely imagination.

"True, but a few days before she killed herself, I ran into her in midtown. I was interviewing at a law firm that just happened to be located on the same floor of the building where a leading gynecologist and obstetrician has an office. When I saw Joan, she was coming out of that doctor's office. She saw me, too, and seemed embarrassed . . . and depressed."

Nickie stared at her beer mug. "You're still surmising a lot, Jack."

"Maybe. But I was so struck by the tragic expression on Joan's face, that after we'd said hello and good-bye, I followed her. Discreetly, of course. She went to a quiet restaurant—Starr was waiting for her there. I managed to get an adjacent booth without either one of them seeing me. They talked in low voices, but I heard enough to confirm my suspicions."

"What exactly did you hear?"

"Joan made a reference to her 'condition.' To symptoms that were 'showing.'"

"And what did Rob say?" Nickie sucked in her breath.

"That one never knew." Jack gave a short, mirthless laugh. "I suppose he was trying to cheer her up with hopes of a miscarriage. That bastard!"

"Did you hear anything else?"

"Joan was crying softly. She said something about having no future. I couldn't hear what Starr replied. At that point, I couldn't take any more. I just wanted to get the hell out of there, and I did. A week later, Joan was dead."

Nickie was numb. "So that's your story?" she said.

"That's my story. As I said, it's not exactly hard evidence. But it fits in—I mean, why the closed inquest? Not to cover up the fact that Joan was a suicide, because the death certificate would become a matter of public record. Evidently, Joan took so many sleeping pills that there was no chance of persuading the medical examiner's office to bring in a verdict of accidental death. So there had to be something else that the Weldons, with their horror of scandal, wanted to hide. I'm convinced that something was Joan's pregnancy."

"But in that case, wouldn't the Weldons have blamed Rob?" Nickie argued. "They didn't bring a lawsuit against him, and I had the impression he still considers them friends. He said he didn't want to discuss Joan's death out of consideration for her parents."

"Even if the Weldons had grounds for a lawsuit, they

wouldn't bring one, nor would they dare have an open rupture with Starr. That would only bring more scandal. Nominally, the Weldons may still be Starr's friends, but the fact is they've been traveling a lot since Joan's death, not seeing much of anybody, including my parents. You can think what you like, make all the excuses for him you want to, but in my book Starr's responsible for Joan's death."

Nickie looked at Jack's twisted features in silence. Finally, she said, "I suppose I ought to thank you for telling me this..."

He shrugged. "Let's not be hypocrites. You're not exactly grateful for the information. But seeing the way you were mooning over Starr on the Fourth, I thought you should know about Joan."

In the ensuing silence, Jack signaled the waitress for the check. Nickie dug mechanically into her purse to pay for her share of the bill.

"Please," Jack said. "My treat—if you can call it that. Believe me, Nickie, I wish you well. You're young and vulnerable, the way Joan was. I don't want your heart-break on my conscience."

"You don't have to worry that I'm going to go home and kill myself." Nickie's laughter was shrill. "You've given me a lot to think about, Jack. Thanks for meeting with me, and for lunch." Like an automaton, she rose and shook hands with him. Then, as fast as her rubbery legs would carry her, she fled toward the loft.

Chapter Ten

"BUT, ROB, I must talk to you!" Nickie twisted the telephone cord around her fingers in frustration. After returning to the loft and mulling over Jack's story, she'd decided the only thing to do was to confront Rob as soon as possible. But he claimed he was too busy to see her either that afternoon or evening.

"Look, darling, if it's about any changes you made in the Bach chapter or the outline, never mind. I'll have Joyce send a messenger to you, and I can look over the new material in the morning on the way to Smalley's."

"Rob, I have to see you before then. It's not about the outline or the Bach chapter."

"Nickie, it will have to wait. If you'd come up this morning—"

"I told you, Jack Naughton asked me to have lunch with him here in the Village. That's what I have to talk to you about."

"Just a minute, Nickie," he said. "Joyce is buzzing me."

He put her on hold, and Nickie began to pace the floor, telephone in hand, as she waited for him to come back on the line.

But when he did, he gave her no opportunity to speak. "Nickie, look, it's the London call I've been waiting for. Louise made the Smalley appointment for eleven, and perhaps we can have lunch afterward and talk then. I'm sorry, but I have to ring off now. Good-bye."

Nickie stood listening to the dial tone for a moment. Then she slammed down the receiver to vent her exasperation. She had to see Rob before the meeting. Perhaps she'd better call Louise and tell her to postpone the appointment with Smalley. She picked up the receiver again and dialed the agent's number.

"Hello, Nickie, have you got the new chapters and the outline for me?" Louise greeted her.

"Yes, Louise, I do, but I was wondering if we could postpone the meeting with Smalley."

"Whatever for, Nickie? Actually, I spoke with Smalley a little while ago. He's found out what Shields is going to say about Joan Weldon and he's quite upset about it. He wants to ask Rob some questions, and I gather that if there's to be any book, Rob will have to answer them. Meanwhile, I've got the contract from Rob's lawyers sitting on my desk. I can't advise you to sign it until we see what this is all about."

"I see your point," Nickie said. "The thing is, I heard something myself about Joan Weldon that I wanted to ask Rob about before the meeting. But perhaps it would be better to hear what Shields is saying and let Smalley confront Rob."

"Absolutely," Louise said. "After all, if there's nothing to it but Shields's lurid imagination, Rob is going to be pretty upset. I wouldn't want him to get furious at *you* and decide to change writers. So let's go ahead with the appointment and play it all by ear, okay?"

"That might be best," Nickie agreed. "I'll bring the

Bach chapter and the outline up to your office right away. Will you be there?"

"I may be with someone, but you can always leave the envelope with my secretary. Oh, here's the writer I was expecting. I'll see you tomorrow, Nickie."

At ten minutes to eleven the next morning, Nickie entered the offices of the Smalley Publishing Company. Louise was already in the outer reception room, looking as elegant as always in a teal-blue designer suit, and Nickie was glad she'd worn a dressy red-and-white striped shirtwaist dress herself.

"Rob called to say he'd be a few minutes late," Louise reported. "Fortunately, I've never known Richard Smalley to start a meeting punctually."

"I suppose Rob got tied up with the big oil deal he's been negotiating," Nickie mused.

"He didn't say. Who knows? Maybe like us ordinary mortals, he simply overslept for a change. I imagine he had a late night, considering this morning's *Post*. Did you see the picture, Nickie?"

"What picture?" Nickie asked, wondering what Louise was talking about.

"This one." Louise unzipped her briefcase and took out a copy of the *Post*. She quickly found the page she was looking for and held it out to Nickie.

Nickie stared at the photograph of Rob and actress Anita Fullbright smiling at each other across a table at some posh restaurant. Her eyes fell to the caption: "Tycoon T. R. Starr seen at Maxwell's Plum last night with old flame Anita Fullbright. Is the much-married actress hitching Starr to her nuptial wagon this time?"

So, he'd been too busy to see her last night, but he'd had time for a leisurely dinner with Anita Fullbright. Of course, Nickie remembered, the actress had called Rob, but he had assured Nickie he'd tell Anita he was otherwise occupied. So much for Rob Starr's assurances.

Had their lovemaking only been a one-night stand for him, Nickie wondered, overwhelmed with hurt and anger. She recalled how ill-at-ease Rob had seemed the morning after they'd made love, but she had attributed that to the subject of their interview, the awkward circumstances. Yet if Jack Naughton's story were true, Starr was such a cad when it came to women that he wouldn't think twice about using a nobody like Nickie Monroe.

"It's a good thing you got Rob to talk at length about Anita," Louise was saying. "Perhaps you should meet with her and get her to give you some quotes about him for the biography."

"Perhaps I'll do that," Nickie said, trying to seem casual as she handed the newspaper back to Louise. What would the agent think if she knew Nickie had made the same mistake with Starr that she'd made with Gregory Thompson. Or had she? If she hadn't heard Jack's story, would she be so quick to think the worst about Rob and Anita, Nickie asked herself. The shade of Joan Weldon was a barrier between them, and Nickie fervently hoped the coming interview would dispel it once and for all.

The receptionist announced that Mr. Smalley would see them, just as Rob walked through the door. Nickie's breath caught in her throat when she saw how handsome he looked in his three-piece charcoal-gray suit and a patterned tie of blue and burnt orange that complemented his brilliant eyes and chestnut hair. He smiled at her so winningly that she almost forgot everything but the way her heart reacted to that smile. But when he whispered, "I've missed you," in her ear as they followed Louise into the publisher's office, Nickie recalled how he'd made time for Anita Fullbright and not for her and was again filled with doubts.

Richard Smalley was a stout, gray-haired man in his fifties, with sharp gray eyes behind rimless glasses. After greeting Louise warmly, he acknowledged the introductions to Rob and Nickie with a smile before sitting back down behind a desk cluttered with piles of manuscripts and loose papers.

"I've been looking forward to meeting you, Mr. Starr," he said.

"It's Nickie Monroe you should be interested in," Rob replied, smiling at Nickie in a way that once more made her want to believe in him. "She's the one who's writing the book."

"True." Richard Smalley looked at Nickie. "I was very impressed with those first two chapters Louise sent me, and even more impressed with the third chapter and outline I read last night, Ms. Monroe. You have a fine career ahead of you as a writer." He paused, templing his fingers precisely. "Mr. Starr, I understand that you've refused to cooperate with Burton Shields on his biography, although you are cooperating fully with Miss Monroe. Is that correct?"

Rob nodded, his lips pressed together in a narrow line of contempt at the mention of Shields's name.

"Then it's the writer you object to, not the biography?" Smalley asked, his eyes sharp. "Excuse the questions, but I want to be sure I understand the situation," he added.

"I'd prefer no biography at all," Rob stated, "but if there's going to be one, I want it to reveal the truth, not a compilation of gossip and rumors."

"Ms. Monroe has already spoken to people who aren't particularly friendly to you," Smalley pointed out, "and will no doubt continue to do so. How can I be sure you won't hinder her, or at some point capriciously decide to call off the book?"

Rob waved a hand in dismissal and gave a lopsided grin. "I'm giving Ms. Monroe free rein. She knows the difference between fact and fiction."

Smalley smiled. "I can understand your point of view. I happen to have a low opinion of Shields myself, and I admit a biography of you appeals to me. You're rich, controversial, romantic. I have no doubt that a book would do well, especially since it would benefit from any publicity that Shields's book gets."

Rob shifted uneasily in his chair at the mention of publicity. "I don't know why you want to speak to me. Nickie here—"

"Is the writer, I know." Smalley picked up a sheaf of papers that Nickie recognized as her outline.

Frowning apprehensively, she glanced at Rob. She knew what Smalley was leading up to, and she also knew that Rob would not like it. Rob, however, smiled at her, seemingly pleased with the conversation.

"I take it you've seen the outline," Smalley said to Rob.

"He has," Louise put in quickly, "and he doesn't object to it." She smiled tentatively at Nickie in reassurance. "Of course, it's only an outline."

Smalley put the papers down to take off his glasses and rub the bridge of his nose. "To be frank, I have a problem with it. I realize that the Weldon incident—"

"No!" Rob's voice was harsher than Nickie had heard it. "It's all gossip, innuendo. The stories were hard enough on Frank and Anne then. To dredge it up now would only hurt them all over again."

"Mr. Starr, personally I sympathize." Smalley put his glasses on again. "But Shields has no such inhibitions. Yesterday his agent called me and asked if I would like to see a partial manuscript of Shields's book. The agent is planning to conduct an auction among hardcover houses on the basis of what Shields has written so far."

"I'm surprised you were called, Richard," Louise remarked. "Shields isn't exactly the sort of author one associates with your firm."

Smalley gave a wry chuckle. "True, but I suppose precisely because of Shields's questionable name, the book would have more credibility if a reputable publisher bought the manuscript—or at least bid on it. Anyway, I said I'd take a look, and I brought the Shields manuscript home with me last night along with Ms. Monroe's chapters, to compare the two. The accounts of your youth, Mr. Starr, differ primarily in slant and emphasis. Shields, of course, paints you as ruthlessly competitive practically from the cradle."

"That doesn't surprise me," Rob said with a grimace. "Go on, Mr. Smalley."

"Well, Shields is a master of innuendo and distortion. His version of the Bach takeover, when contrasted with Ms. Monroe's, shows how clever he can be at twisting the facts. I'm sure he's manipulated the truth in the same way when it comes to Joan Weldon, but I had no basis for comparison there."

"Richard, perhaps you'd just better tell us what Shields has to say about Joan Weldon straight out," Louise suggested quietly.

"Very well." The publisher looked uncomfortable. "It's not a pretty tale. In brief, he suggests that the young woman killed herself because you, Mr. Starr, got her pregnant and then refused to marry her."

Nickie sucked in her breath. So Shields was telling the same story Jack had told her—and Jack had said he hadn't spoken to Shields, had never even heard of him. "Mr. Smalley," she said, hoping her voice was steadier than she felt, "did Shields have any hard evidence for his allegations?"

"Not exactly, Ms. Monroe," the publisher conceded, "and I'm certain no publisher will let him go as far as he does in libeling Mr. Starr." He turned to Rob. "He even accuses you of planting the idea of suicide in the young woman's head, although after reading the manuscript closely I saw nothing but conjecture to back that statement up. He does, however, provide some documentation for the rest of his story. He's talked to a number of men who had asked Joan Weldon for dates and were rebuffed. She told them all she was seeing you exclusively. To some she confided that she was in love with you."

"Does he name the men?" Louise asked.

"Yes, he does," Smalley replied, "and they're all very solid individuals. That's what differentiates these allegations from others in the manuscript. And he's got more evidence of Joan's pregnancy. The most convincing statement came from a well-known society matron. A few days before Joan's death, this woman was in the waiting room of a midtown gynecologist when Joan came out of the doctor's office. Shields quotes the woman as saying that Joan looked 'haunted.'"

Rob's features were impassive. "Is that it?" he asked stiffly.

"Not quite. Most damning of all is the statement Shields produces from a waiter who served you and Joan at the restaurant you took her to for dinner after the theater on the night she died. The man says he overheard Joan begging you to marry her and take her away somewhere, 'so no one will ever know'—presumably, so no one would know she'd been pregnant at the time of the marriage. You're reputed to have said, 'We've been through all this before, Joan, and this isn't the place to discuss it again. Let me take you home.'"

Smalley fell silent. Starr seemed to become conscious that they were all waiting for him to speak. He cleared his throat and said, "As usual, Shields has put two and two together and made five."

"Are you willing to be quoted on that in Ms. Monroe's biography?" Smalley asked. "Are you willing to tell your own story—that is, whatever you know—about Joan Weldon's death?"

Rob frowned. "When Shields first decided to write the book, he approached the Weldons. Anne Weldon called me, distraught at the idea of the tragedy being raked up all over again, and she asked me to say nothing—absolutely nothing—to anyone about it. I gave her my word."

"Good Lord, man," Louise said impatiently, "you have to say something. Don't you realize that your silence will be taken as an admission of guilt?"

"Not, I hope"—Rob glanced at Nickie—"by those who know me."

"Mr. Starr, perhaps you could talk to the Weldons," Smalley suggested. "They might reconsider once they hear what Shields is saying."

"Yes, Rob," Nickie put in, "it wouldn't hurt to talk to them."

He shook his head. "The Weldons feel that whatever Shields says will bring them a period of unwelcome notoriety, during which time they plan to escape the publicity by taking a cruise. Given the kind of reputation Shields has, they feel the whole thing will die down fairly quickly. Whereas if I start the gossip up all over again . . ."

"Why can't you just tell the truth?" Louise demanded. "At least call the Weldons and try to convince them it would be the best thing to do."

"And if I disagree?" Rob said slowly, looking from Louise to Smalley. "If I simply refuse to say any more about Joan than Nickie has indicated on the outline . . . ?"

Smalley sighed. "Mr. Starr, I consider myself a pretty good judge of character. I believe that your silence is motivated by genuine concern for the Weldons rather than a desire to protect yourself. And I would like to publish Ms. Monroe's biography of you. But I will only do so if you're willing to rebut Shields's story."

"I see. Thank you for your time and opinion . . . and your vote of confidence." Rob rose and shook the publisher's hand. "I need some time to consider. I'll be going to London for a few days on business. How about if I call Louise next week, after I get back, and she passes my decision on to you?"

"That will be fine. I do hope you'll decide to set the record straight, Mr. Starr, and not only because I want to publish the book."

Nickie looked at Louise. "I have some other business to discuss with Richard, Nickie," the agent said. "I'll phone you later, from my office."

"Fine," Nickie agreed, sensing that Louise wished her to leave with Rob and use her powers of persuasion to convince him to talk to the Weldons. "It was good to meet you, Mr. Smalley," she told the publisher as she rose to her feet.

Smalley stood also, and warmly shook her hand. "I look forward to working with you, Ms. Monroe." He glanced at Rob. "Either on this book or another one."

When they had left the publisher's office and were outside in the elevator area, Rob put a hand on Nickie's arm. "We'll have lunch . . . and talk?" he suggested.

"Yes, we have to talk," she agreed. They said no more as they rode the elevator to the lobby together. Then, putting an arm around Nickie's waist, Rob led her to the street and said, "The Algonquin is just a block away. Would you like to eat there?"

"Fine," Nickie replied. At any other time, she would have been thrilled by the prospect of lunch at the famed hotel where Dorothy Parker and other members of the *New Yorker* "Round Table" had gathered to exchange witty repartee. But today, neither the hotel's elegant Old World decor nor the glimpses she had of various literary and theatrical celebrities lifted Nickie's spirits in the least. The time had come for a showdown with Rob. Not only the biography, but their entire relationship was at stake.

The maître d' instantly recognized Rob and whisked them to a table. Nickie barely listened to the niceties Rob exchanged with their waiter, who—like the maître d'—treated the tycoon with utmost deference. As soon as the man had taken their order and left, Nickie took a deep breath and began to speak. "Rob, this afternoon wasn't the first time I heard that Joan Weldon was in love with you—or that she killed herself because she was carrying your child and you wouldn't marry her. Jack Naughton told me the same thing at lunch yesterday. That's what I wanted to talk to you about last night."

He looked at her steadily across the table. "Nickie, would you believe Jack Naughton's word against mine?"

"That's not the issue!"

"Isn't it? Jack's younger than I am, good-looking, and you certainly couldn't find nicer in-laws than Grace and John Naughton."

She stared at him. "What on earth are you talking about?"

"About your date with Jack Naughton."

"It wasn't a date!"

"You mean you were interviewing Jack for the book?" he said hopefully.

"Well, not exactly," she admitted. "The fact is, Jack thought he should, well, as he put it, 'warn' me about you."

"Because he's interested in you and wants to beat out the competition!"

"No. There's no attraction of that kind on either side, Rob."

"No? Then if that isn't it, and if it wasn't for the book, why did he feel the need to 'warn' you?" he asked ironically.

"Because he was afraid I was falling in love with you," Nickie said, then flushed and lowered her eyes to the table.

"Nickie, look at me," Rob said softly. When she kept her gaze on the tablecloth, he said, "I won't embarrass you by asking if it's true. At least not before telling you that I've fallen in love with you."

Instantly, she looked up at him, and saw only sincerity and a kind of anxious appeal in his eyes.

"I didn't plan to tell you this here . . . now," he said,

"but you're the first woman since Jessie I've really fallen for. I love you, Nickie. I wanted to say it the night we made love, but you wouldn't let me. Maybe it's better that I say it here, while we're sitting together like this, because then you'll know that I really mean it."

"Oh, Rob . . ." For a moment, the joy that flooded through her swept away all other emotions. But quickly her euphoria was clouded with doubt and suspicion. If he had wanted to distract her from thinking about Joan Weldon, he had found a surefire way to do it.

The sommelier approached with the bottle of Burgundy Rob had ordered before she could say anything further. Rob went through the ritual of tasting the wine and approving it, and the wine steward filled their glasses and left. But before Nickie could say a word, Rob began to speak again.

"Darling, I have a confession to make. I was annoyed with you yesterday when you said you couldn't come to the penthouse because you were having lunch with Jack. I jumped to the wrong conclusions, and I was, well, jealous. So I called Anita Fullbright and asked her to dinner, even though I'd told her Wednesday that I was too busy to get together. I deliberately took her to a restaurant where I thought we'd be photographed, so that you'd be jealous."

"I did see the picture in the *Post*," Nickie told him, "but, Rob—"

"I took her home right after dinner, Nickie," he assured her. "Oh, and by the way—I told Anita about the book and she said she'd love to be interviewed for it."

"Rob, is there going to be any book?"

The question hung in the air between them as the waiter brought their plates of roast prime ribs au jus and Yorkshire pudding. It seemed like an eternity to Nickie before he left them alone again.

"Is there going to be any book?" she repeated.

Rob attacked his roast beef savagely. "There are other

publishers besides Smalley."

"And they'll all say the same thing," Nickie told him. "But that's really not the point, Rob. You haven't said Shields's story is a total fabrication—and Jack corroborated it. He saw Joan coming out of the doctor's office. He followed her to a restaurant afterward where she met you and overheard some conversation between you. It's all very well to tell Smalley you'll think things over, but I can't go on with the biography—or with anything else— until I know the truth about you and Joan Weldon."

He looked at her with anguished eyes. "Nickie, you've got to believe I wasn't responsible for her suicide. That's all I feel at liberty to say, even to you, darling. I feel so damn helpless, I . . . Look, I'll talk to the Weldons as soon as I get back from London—I mean, as soon as *we* get back from London. You will go with me, won't you?"

Her heart lifted. Rob's willingness to talk to the Weldons seemed proof that he had nothing to be ashamed of in his conduct toward Joan. He hadn't merely been prevaricating in Smalley's office.

"Rob, couldn't you talk to the Weldons right away? Before London?"

"There isn't time. I have a million things to do this afternoon, tomorrow. The thing is, I was hoping we could go tomorrow night, sleep on the flight, and have some time together on Sunday, before I have any meetings. I'm afraid things will be pretty hectic later, like they were in Curaçao, although I'll make all the time for you I can, Nickie. And I'll give you more information for the book."

"I've never been to London," she said, feeling excited about the trip despite her doubts.

"Good. I'll enjoy being the one to show it to you. Nickie . . ." He gave her a searching look. "I've told you my feelings, but you haven't yet said how you feel about me."

She was touched by his vulnerability. It was hard to

believe that she could be the cause of any feelings of insecurity in this man who had everything. She forgot all else but her desire to reassure him.

"I love you, Rob," she said softly. "It's just—"

"No justs, or buts, or any other qualifications," he said gaily, taking her hand and giving it an intimate squeeze. "And as soon as this damn biography is finished, we're going to be married!"

Chapter Eleven

AS SHE SHOPPED frantically on Saturday, spending a large portion of the advance from the biography on clothes for London, Nickie felt as if she were buying her bridal trousseau. And in a way she was, she thought, smiling to herself. There was no doubt in her mind now about the sincerity of Rob's love, which he had reinforced with myriad caresses and endearments once they had left the Algonquin and he had driven her back to the loft in his Mercedes.

But, elated as she was, Nickie had to admit to herself that the mystery of Joan Weldon was still nagging at her. Her happiness would not be unalloyed until that ghost was laid to rest once and for all. An inner voice told her that for all his busy schedule, Rob might have found the time to speak to the Weldons before their departure, if he had really wanted to. Perhaps she should try to persuade him to call them from London. No, Nickie chided herself, she must be patient and not bring up the subject

during their trip. Rob had made it an issue of trust between them, and if she pursued it, seemed to doubt his
word, she might lose his love forever.

They had agreed that Rob's limousine would call for
her Saturday night at eight o'clock, and she was all packed
and waiting for the ring from the lobby that came just
before the hour. When she opened the door a few minutes
later, expecting Burns, Rob himself was there. With bell-
boy courtesy and a twinkle in his eye, he asked, "Luggage, ma'am?"

Nickie laughed and handed him the suitcase. "I suppose you expect a tip."

"Now that you mention it . . ." He put the suitcase
down. In the next instant, he had her in his arms, hugging
her as his mouth closed down on hers in a passionate
kiss, crushing her lips with a promise of joy to come.

"Rob!" she gasped breathlessly, when he finally released her.

"A tip in advance always ensures better service," he
said lightly, his words loaded with intimacy.

Nickie could feel herself flushing. He gave her no
chance to respond, however, as he picked up the suitcase
and headed for the elevator, leaving her behind to lock
the door.

On the drive to Teterboro Airport, he behaved dec-
orously, but Nickie knew that was because of Burns. The
plane took off as soon as they boarded, and the steward
served them a light dinner with wine. Then Rob suggested they sing for a while as they had done on the
flight to Curaçao. This time, Nickie wholeheartedly joined
Rob in one romantic duet after another, and in a lovely
trance put her arms around his neck as he carried her to
the plane's sleeping quarters.

She didn't awaken until Rob gently shook her shoulder
to announce that they were landing at Gatwick Airport.
Nickie's watch said 5 A.M., which meant it was 10 A.M.
London time. She forced herself to get up and dress, but

was asleep on her feet as they departed from the plane and went through customs. She dozed on Rob's shoulder throughout the forty-five-minute taxi ride to central London.

"You really are a sleepyhead," he murmured affectionately as the taxi deposited them at the Dorchester Hotel opposite the green expanse of Hyde Park.

"Who, me? I'm wide awake," she said stubbornly, blinking her eyes rapidly as they entered the lobby of the hotel.

As in Curaçao, the manager was waiting for them. Tail-coated and properly British, he showed them to their rooms. Rob had a suite and Nickie the room across the hall. Again, too, there were flowers, and a bowl of fruit and cheese in the suite, in addition to a well-stocked bar.

"Shall I have breakfast sent up, or let you get in a few more hours of shut-eye first?" Rob asked her solicitously.

"Breakfast. I'll be fine once I've had a cup of coffee," Nickie said, but her words were belied by a sleepy yawn.

"I don't think so, little one. It's all right; I have some paper work to take care of anyway." Tenderly, he deposited her on the bed in her room, planting butterfly kisses on her hair, her neck, her ears.

"Rob . . ."

"Just catch up on your sleep, Nickie. I should have sent you to bed earlier last night on the plane. I forgot you're not as used to all this jetting around as I am."

She fell into a dreamless sleep, and was awakened hours later by Rob knocking at her door.

"What time is it?" she asked, now wide awake.

He kissed her briefly on the lips. "Tea time," he said, ushering her across the hall to his suite, where a tea caddy awaited them replete with silver teapot and plates of tiny sandwiches, delicate cakes, and warm scones wrapped up in linen napkins.

"Goodness, I'm starving," Nickie said as Rob loaded

a plate with delicacies for her. Feeling very much the *grande dame,* she poured the tea. "Lemon or cream and sugar?" she asked him.

He grinned. "Don't you remember my preference for sweet things?"

Nickie laughed as she took the silver sugar tongs and sweetened his tea. She put lemon in her own cup. "Rob, I'm sorry I slept through our day of sightseeing," she said contritely.

"It's only four o'clock," he said good-naturedly, then bit into a wafer-thin cucumber sandwich. "We have time for a stroll to Trafalgar Square, and from there we can catch a pleasure launch at Westminster."

"You mean we're actually going to sail up the Thames?" Nickie asked, finishing a rich, buttery scone and widening her eyes in delight. "Oh, Rob, I can't believe we're really in London."

She still had to pinch herself to make sure it wasn't a dream as they walked from the hotel to the boat dock, with Rob pointing out landmark after landmark in the gathering dusk. At Victoria Embankment, they boarded the R.S. *Hispaniola,* and, ensconced in luxurious arm-chairs, enjoyed the magnificent view of historic London from Big Ben to St. Paul's as they glided up the Thames. Even more, Nickie enjoyed Rob's witty anecdotes and yearning looks, which found an echo in her own heart. After an excellent Spanish dinner on the boat's upper deck, she gazed in contented silence at the glimmering lights along the riverbank, nestled against Rob's powerful chest as they stood together at the railing.

They spoke little on the taxi ride back to the hotel, and as if by tacit agreement went to Rob's suite for an after-dinner drink. As they sat on the brocade couch sipping Cointreau, Rob's gaze lingered on the décolleté neckline of Nickie's new sundress. When at last he put aside their glasses and drew her into his arms, she was already enflamed with desire for him.

"It's been so long. I've wanted you so these past
days," he murmured, burning a trail of kisses from her
throat to the top of her low-cut dress.

"I've wanted you, too, Rob," she breathed, her breasts
rising against his chest as their lips came together in a
passionate kiss.

Hand in hand, they made their way to the darkened
bedroom. Rob cupped Nickie's face in his hands and
gazed at her in silent wonder. He stroked her jaw with
his thumb and outlined her full lips, then touched his
mouth to hers. He kissed her lightly, savoring the taste
of her and exploring the shape of her lips. His tongue
lingered on hers before his lips moved to her eyelids and
throbbing temples. Just when she yearned most for him
to do so, he fused his mouth with hers again, demanding
more and more of her. She gave him everything he wanted.

Rob's slow and delicate touch was arousing Nickie in
ways she had never before experienced. One by one, her
senses were coming to life, as if from a long sleep. They
stirred faintly and began to hum with awareness. As Rob
unbuttoned her sundress and slid it carefully off her
shoulders, kissing and caressing every inch of flesh he
exposed, Nickie's senses came fully alive, clamoring to
be heard. She gasped when he covered her breast with
the palm of his hand and took her taut, aching nipple
into his mouth. A crescendo of need arose inside her to
a vibrant, feverish pitch.

"Nickie, darling, I love you so much," Rob said
hoarsely as he removed the rest of her clothes and skimmed
his hand over her naked body in a way that made her
stretch and arch like a cat being stroked. She threw back
her head in total abandon, throbbing, burning with desire.

Restlessly she moved against him, her own hands now
eager on his body, seeking their own discoveries. Abruptly
she stripped the shirt from his chest and tangled her
fingers in his matted hair, then stroked the sinewy muscles. "I love you, Rob," she said breathlessly. Her mouth

followed her hand down his torso, tracing the line of hair that thinned and disappeared into his trousers. Frustrated by this obstruction, she unbuckled his belt with trembling fingers and, fired by a new urgency, unzipped his pants and pulled them from his lean hips.

She knelt before him and buried her face in his stomach. He groaned and gripped her arms to pull her up to him. "Nickie, Nickie," he murmured hoarsely, "I need you—now." He kissed her long and hard, his tongue filling her mouth and moving rhythmically against hers.

Then he was urging her down across the bed and falling beside her, his rock-hard form, now naked, pressed intimately against her. How she welcomed the full weight of him pushing her into the bedclothes! How she reveled in his hardness molding against her softness. She felt enveloped by him.

"You have such lovely breasts," Rob whispered. He paid homage to them with tender fingers, then searing lips. "I love all of you." Gently his hands parted her thighs, and he touched her most intimately. Stroking her to full readiness, he drew nearer to the very center of her desire. As she caressed him in return, she was overwhelmed with a wondrous sense of intimacy. And when he joined his body to hers, murmuring words of love, she felt both consumed and released. Self-awareness was annihilated as they moved together, slowly at first, then faster and faster, drawing closer and closer to an earth-shattering climax.

Nickie gasped. Her breath came fast and shallow. For one suspended moment the world seemed to spin away. And then she was spiraling into a vortex of pleasure as Rob brought her to a shuddering release a moment before his own. They lay panting together, their hearts racing.

For long, rapturous minutes they lay fused one to the other, their blood cooling, their breath calming. At last, in a rosy afterglow of love, Nickie fell asleep in Rob's

arms, her thought being that she had never felt so ful-
filled, so totally a woman.

Moments later, it seemed, a telephone rang in the
distance and stopped. Then a hand was shaking her shoulder. Nickie forced her eyes open. Rob, dressed in a terry-
cloth robe, his hair wet from the shower, was smiling
down at her. Seeing that she was awake, he sat beside
her, his eyes filled with tenderness as he kissed her gently
on the lips. Her body roused, and her arms went around
his neck. They held one another, wonder at the joy of
the night bringing them closer than ever.

"I don't remember when I've ever slept so well, or
had such lovely dreams," he murmured in her ear.

Nickie smiled with pleasure. She stretched, luxuriat-
ing in the pull of her muscles. Rob grinned and handed
her a robe. "I can't believe my sleepyhead is up at seven,"
he said.

"It makes a difference when I sleep in your arms,"
she teased. Kissing the firm line of his jaw, she added,
"I had lovely dreams, too."

"And now breakfast is waiting for you," he said, holding her close as they walked into the living room.

The dining table had been removed in favor of a breakfast table, laid for two. Under the silver covers of the
serving dishes was a typically English breakfast: eggs
with two rashers of bacon, sausages, a broiled tomato,
and a broiled kipper. Slices of toast stood in a silver rack
beside bowls of honey and marmalade and a big pot of
coffee.

"What are your plans for today?" Nickie asked, as
they ate.

"Meetings all day, I'm afraid," Rob said regretfully,
buttering a slice of toast carefully and then spreading it
with marmalade. "But, thank God, British businessmen
are more civilized than we Americans. I can guarantee
that I'll be back at the hotel by seven, in time to take

you to dinner at the Savoy." A note of anxiety in his voice, he added, "Until then, darling, will it seem all too reminiscent of Curaçao if I suggest you take a sight-seeing tour?"

"There was no Savoy in Curaçao," she teased, thinking of how many things had changed since that time.

His face cleared and they laughed together. "Is it only the Savoy you're looking forward to?" he asked slyly.

"If you have to ask, you don't deserve an answer," she twitted him as she sprinkled her tomato with salt.

"Still as snippy as ever." He shook his head in mock despair. "What am I going to do with you?"

"Well, if you didn't have to run off to those boring old meetings, I'm sure I could come up with an idea or two."

"Just keep them in mind until tonight. We could even skip the Savoy," Rob added wickedly. He grinned as he finished his toast and took a final sip of coffee. "I'd better dress," he said reluctantly. "Take your time with breakfast. Think about what you'd like to see today."

"I'd rather think about you," she told him fondly, and was indeed still recalling the pleasures of the previous night when he emerged from the bedroom a few minutes later, dressed in an elegant tan suit and carrying his briefcase.

"We who are about to die of boredom salute you," he greeted her. "I'm really tempted to play hookey and go sightseeing with you, Nickie."

"Perish the thought!" she cried, though she was delighted he'd said it. "How would I explain *that* in the biography? One kiss, and then off with you."

"One long kiss," he amended. But though they savored each other's lips to the fullest, the kiss wasn't half long enough for either of them.

Nevertheless, the warmth of Rob's lips seemed to sustain her as she set off to see the sights of London, which she elected to do in her own independent fashion rather than joining an organized tour. It was a beautiful sunny day, and she decided to take advantage of the cloudless sky—which her guidebook suggested was most rare for London—by meandering through Hyde Park.

The lawns were a lush vibrant green, with trees casting pools of shade over couples reclining lazily in the grass. More industrious souls rowed lustily across the Serpentine Lake, which ran the width of the park. Nickie followed paths flanked by colorful flowers to Rotten Row, where in Victorian and Edwardian times, the gentry had paraded on horseback and in carriages to see and be seen by promenaders and each other: in her imagination, Nickie saw them in their glory and almost heard the clip-clop of their horses. She left the park and walked down Knightsbridge to Brompton Road with its elegant department stores and shops. She passed up Mark & Spencer's for Harrod's, where she paused to admire the windows and flower boxes with their perky geraniums that graced the sedate yellow stone façade.

Inside the store, she marveled not only at the sheer volume and diversity of merchandise, but also at the artistic displays in each department. Feeling somewhat unpatriotic, she thought to herself that Bloomingdale's and Macy's could learn a thing or two from their British counterpart. In the fashionable women's department she began to regret having already refurbished her wardrobe in New York.

Strolling through the men's department, she stopped on impulse to buy Rob a cream-colored tie patterned with bright crimson strawberries. Later, as she lunched on fish and chips in the Green Man, a pub located right inside Harrod's, she wondered if Rob might not think her gift rather corny. But when she shyly presented it to him that evening as they relaxed over pre-dinner cocktails in his suite, he seemed genuinely tickled with the gift.

"Do you know, you're the first woman ever to buy me a present," he told her, "not to mention how much

I love this one in particular." His face was flushed with pleasure, making his eyes seem even bluer than usual.

"I find that hard to believe," Nickie said. "I mean, not even for your birthday, or Christmas?"

"Cross my heart," he told her. "Almost always, I've been invited to dinner on such occasions, or given a humorous card to the effect that there's nothing to give the man who has everything. You don't know how this touches me, Nickie. I only wish I had something to give you right now in return."

"Oh, but what could you give the woman who has the man who has everything?" she asked lightly.

"For starters, I wish I could give him to you all the time," he replied ruefully. "I'm afraid tomorrow is going to be another long day of meetings. Perhaps even longer than today."

"Well, we'll just have to make the most of tonight, then," she said brightly, although she felt a stab of disappointment. The afternoon had seemed longer than the morning. Thoughts of Rob had distracted her from the Beefeater guide's speech during the tour of the Tower she had elected to go on; and even as she'd admired the Crown Jewels, she had to admit that, for all their magnificence, she'd rather be looking at the sparkle in Rob's eyes.

A memorable dinner of chateaubriand with pommes soufflés for two and champagne, followed by peach melba—which had been invented by the Savoy's most renowned chef, Escoffier—did much to lift Nickie's spirits again. And a second night in Rob's arms—a night of pleasuring each other in their own special Eden of love—left her with an inner radiance that took the edge off the following day of lonely sightseeing in the City, London's financial district, and the National Gallery.

That evening, as they shared a late supper in the revolving restaurant at Top of the Tower, which offered a breathtaking panorama of London as well as first-rate

Belgian cuisine, Rob announced that he had good news.

"No meetings until late afternoon tomorrow. So at least we can see Westminster Abbey and the Changing of the Guard together."

"I was rather saving them on the off-chance," she confessed as they smiled into one another's eyes.

The next morning, after a sumptuous breakfast in Rob's suite, they set off for Westminster Abbey. Nickie's heart swelled as they stood in the nave and gazed around at the majestic interior of the Abbey. Tattered battle flags hung from the Gothic arches, and underfoot the flag-stones were as smooth as satin, worn down over the centuries by millions of feet. The previous day, during her excursion to the City, she had visited London's other famous church, St. Paul's Cathedral. Yet that awesome testament to Sir Christopher Wren's architectural genius had inspired her with a mere intellectual appreciation, while the abbey filled her spirit with a sense of partici-pation in all of Britain's history.

With his arm about her waist, Rob guided her around the vast shrine, where the majority of Britain's monarchs had been crowned and the bones of many rested in elab-orate chapels, along with the relics of such illustrious personages as Lord Nelson and the Duchess of Rich-mond, whose wax image Nickie recognized as the sym-bolic figure of Britannia from the British penny.

"And last but not least, here's Poet's Corner," Rob said as they paused before the monuments to Britain's literary giants.

"My goodness, they go back all the way to Chaucer," Nickie said, awed.

"Yes, and don't overlook the tomb of our compatriot, Henry Wadsworth Longfellow," Rob told her, pointing it out.

From the Westminster Abbey they strolled arm in arm through St. James's Park to Buckingham Palace. It was only a quarter to eleven, but already a sizable crowd had gathered to await the Changing of the Guard at eleven-thirty.

"There will probably be a better view at the Whitehall Ceremony—fewer tourists know about it," Rob said. "And the Changing of the Guard there is equally spectacular."

"Lead the way," Nickie replied gaily, far from averse to another promenade on Rob's arm. She cast a last look at the splendid palace and the red-jacketed sentries with their tall beaver hats standing immobile in front of the sentry boxes, then glanced up at the gathering clouds that had blocked out the sun.

"I hope it's not going to rain," she remarked.

"Not during the Changing of the Guard—I won't allow it," Rob said grandly as they made their way to the far side of the park and Whitehall. Nickie noticed that a number of women gave more than a cursory glance to Rob's tall, athletic form, and Nickie even thought she detected some looks of envy in her own direction.

The crowd at the gold-tipped iron gates of Whitehall was less dense than at the palace, and Rob maneuvered them to a spot with an excellent view of the pageant, which began shortly after they arrived. Nickie was deliciously aware of the feathery kisses Rob was planting on the top of her head and the base of her neck just above the collar of her violet silk dress, but she kept her eyes focused on the mounted guards in the boxes on either side of the gates to the courtyard. She was struck by the way the black horse with the white star on its forehead remained virtually motionless except for a nod of its head now and then or a stamp of a white-stockinged hoof, while the man on its back seemed to be a statue in his high-necked blue uniform jacket. The embossed metal helmet almost touched the bridge of his nose in front, and the plume at the crest barely moved in the slight breeze that had sprung up.

An officer appeared with two other mounted guards in red jackets. On command from the officer on foot, the blue-jacketed guards rode out of their boxes and solemnly walked into the courtyard. In the meantime, they were replaced by the men in red, while the officer inspected the relieved guards, first mounted and then on foot. To Nickie's amusement, once dismounted, the guards seemed to lose some of their somber majesty to become ordinary men, a little short and plump. The inspection over, the officer barked a command, then marched the guards through an archway into the inner recesses of Whitehall.

"Come on," Rob said, glancing toward the sky where lowering clouds were turning black. "There's one more stop we have to make."

Puzzled, Nickie let him lead her down Whitehall to a narrow street at the corner. A sign high up on the wall informed her that the cobblestoned passage, more like a dead-end alley, was Downing Street. The buildings fronted directly on a ribbon of sidewalk, and halfway down it were a few steps leading to a plain wooden door with a simple brass knocker, above which was an inconspicuous number 10. On either side stood a uniformed London bobby, hands clasped casually behind his back.

"It's not very fancy, is it?" Rob mused.

"Well, the prime minister isn't royalty," Nickie replied, recalling the pomp at Whitehall, the splendor of the queen's guards at Buckingham Palace, and the Elizabethan grandeur of the Beefeaters.

A splatter of rain made Rob say, "Uh-oh. Let's see if we can find a cab before we get soaked."

Nickie smiled, not at all surprised when Rob flagged one down almost immediately. She had to step high to enter the roomy interior, with Rob behind her. As she settled back on the hard leather bench, he leaned forward to direct the driver to Beauchamps Place.

"There's a typically English pub there that I think

you'll like," Rob told her. "If the rain keeps up, we have a choice of good restaurants nearby for lunch, too." He looked at her with a smile that lit the depths of his blue eyes.

After weaving its way past Victoria Station, the cab turned down a series of small streets that made Nickie lose all sense of direction. If Rob had not told her that London cabbies were the best in the world, that they had to pass a stringent test on their knowledge of the city, she would have been sure they were lost. Finally, at the corner of a narrow, shop-lined street, bumper to bumper with cars in the rain, he told the driver to stop.

After he had paid the fare and helped Nickie out of the cab, Rob explained, "We can walk it faster if you don't mind a little rain."

He hurried her past a Georgian house to a pub next door. The pub was actually two rooms separated by a bar that permitted the people behind it to serve both sides, both of which were crowded. A few old-fashioned sewing-machine stands with tabletops lined the walls, and several stools graced the bar. Most of the floor space and all of the seats were taken by cheerful knots of people holding pints or half-pints of beer or ale. Rob elbowed his way to the bar and returned shortly with two half-pints.

Nickie sipped the cool, bitter brew thirstily. "It's good," she acknowledged, forced to shout above the noise in the pub.

Rob frowned at the surrounding din and said, "There's a small room upstairs. Let's go there."

Nickie nodded and followed him through the bar to a steep flight of stairs that turned sharply back on itself to a small room with tables and a small bar at one end. The blond barmaid smiled at them, as Nickie sank gratefully onto a bench at one of the booths by the windows overlooking Beauchamps Place. "I thought I walked a lot in New York," she exclaimed, "but that's nothing compared to the past three days." She slipped her pumps off to wriggle her toes.

Rob smiled, his eyes warm with admiration. "You look as fresh as a daisy. That may not be very original, but it's true."

"And you look tired," she observed, noting the circles under his eyes and the sharply drawn lines of his face. "Perhaps instead of taking me sightseeing, you should have spent the morning resting at the hotel before your afternoon meetings."

"And not have any chance at all to see London with you? Never! I only regret that we can't stay on a few days more, but I'm afraid we'll have to fly back to New York tonight. This afternoon should wrap up the deal, and I've got a thousand things to take care of at home."

His sincerity touched Nickie and brought a glow to her cheeks. "This might be a good time to catch me up on what you've been doing over here," she suggested.

"My biographer." Rob grinned and blew her a kiss that implied how much more to him she was than that.

As they sipped their beers, Rob launched into the topic of drilling for oil and the dangers of sea exploration from tides and storms. Nickie listened, fascinated by his knowledge, only half aware of the rain now pelting against the windows and dampening the drooping geraniums in the windowboxes of the buildings across the street.

Finally he paused, giving a short laugh. "I must be boring you." He glanced out the window. "Do you feel like a quick run next door? There's an excellent Italian restaurant in the basement."

"I am hungry," Nickie admitted.

"Then let's make a dash for it," Rob suggested.

He led the way next door and down a narrow, winding staircase to a chic little restaurant. Separating a small square room with banquettes and a narrow room with tables along the walls was a small bar and a buffet table laid out with fresh lobster and fish. The waiter seated them at a table for two and handed them the menus, which were written on long scrolls. Rob immediately suggested a cold lobster mayonnaise with champagne to start, followed by spaghetti Bolognese and a salad.

As soon as the waiter had brought the champagne and poured it, Rob held up his glass. "To London, Nickie. I'm sorry the trip has been so short and hectic. You've been such a sport about my leaving you alone during the day."

"You were afraid I'd complain—the way Jessie did in Paris," Nickie guessed. "But we've had such wonderful evenings."

"I meant to take you to the theater one night," he said with a rueful smile.

Nickie felt the woodenness of her answering smile. At his mention of the theater, the image of Joan Weldon had risen, unbidden, in her mind. The heiress had killed herself after attending a Broadway opening with Rob.

"Is something wrong, Nickie?" Rob inquired solicitously, reaching across the table to take her hand.

Any answer Nickie might have made was silenced by the arrival of a tall waiter with a drooping mustache who set their lobster in front of them. The bite-size pieces were heaped in their red shells and topped by a homemade mayonnaise with a touch of mustard and dill. The spaghetti that followed was perfectly *al dente* under tasty meat sauce over which the waiter spooned freshly grated parmesan cheese. The salad of mixed greens with a tart oil-and-vinegar dressing was the ideal accompaniment.

Afterward, Rob ordered espresso and cognac. Sighing with contentment, Nickie sipped the bitter, strong coffee. "What time will we be leaving London?" she asked Rob.

"I should be finished with business about six. How do you plan to spend the afternoon?"

"I'll just go back to the hotel and pack, take some notes for the book. If you'll fill me in on the conclusion of the deal on the flight tonight, I can start writing the new chapter tomorrow in New York."

"Nickie, what's your hurry? Honestly, you make me feel like Simon Legree," he teased.

"You were the one who said you couldn't wait for the book to be finished," she reminded him.

"So we could be married." He smiled tenderly at her. "You know, Nickie," he went on, adding another lump of sugar to his espresso, "I've been thinking. Why don't we just forget the book altogether? Then we wouldn't have to wait."

She looked at him searchingly and saw he wasn't joking. She also saw that he wasn't just carried away by love; he looked troubled and uncomfortable. "Rob," she said quietly, "you're not being completely open with me. What is this all about?"

He dropped his eyes to the table and sighed. "I shouldn't have said anything. I planned to wait until we were back in New York. Nickie, I can't call the Weldons and ask them to let me discuss Joan in the biography. It's just impossible." He raised his eyes to hers again and sent her a pleading look. "Darling, please try to understand."

She stared at him incredulously. "You've felt that way all along, haven't you? You lied to me at the Algonquin when you said you'd call them as soon as we returned from London. This whole trip has been nothing but a farce!"

"No!" He took her hands in his. "I love you, Nickie, and I want you to be my wife. I never lied about that. And I asked you to come to London because I wanted to be with you. The time we've spent together here has meant so much to me, darling."

She jerked her hands away. "Don't try to softsoap me, Rob. I know why you wanted me to come to London. You thought you'd show me a good time, all the things your money can buy, and then I'd be too dazzled to think straight when you called off the biography. I trusted you . . ."

"Trust me still," he beseeched her. "I'm sorry for the time you've already put into the biography, but you could always revise the material you have into an article, couldn't you?"

She shook her head in disbelief. "The biography isn't the point, Rob. Don't you understand that? Unless you tell me the truth about Joan Weldon, your secret—whatever it is—would always be between us."

"It's not *my* secret."

"Then why can't you tell me the truth? Until you do, Rob, I'm not going to see you again." She got to her feet. "I mean it, Rob. I'm going back to the hotel to pack, and then I'm taking the first commercial flight to New York I can get from Heathrow. I can't go through any more charades with you. If you love me, you'll tell me the truth. Otherwise, we have nothing more to say to each other."

Chapter Twelve

ONE MORNING A week after she returned to New York, Nickie was just sitting down to her typewriter, determined to blot out the pain of losing Rob by immersing herself in her novel, when someone knocked on the door. Dispiritedly, she went to see who it was, hoping it would only be the exterminator. She was too unhappy to talk to anyone.

She opened the door and stared, stunned. Rob! He was the last person she'd expected. After days of waiting, she'd finally given up all hope of his changing his mind. Now she stood in the doorway drinking in the familiar face, the warm blue eyes, the strawberry tie she had given him.

He smiled with a warmth that melted her heart. "You'll have to dress, too," he said, glancing at her patched jeans and faded workshirt. "Not that you don't look ravishing to me whatever you wear, but it will seem strange if I show up in a suit and tie and you come like that. Fortunately, we're not expected until eleven, so that gives you time to get ready."

"Get ready for what, Rob?" she asked warily. "You mean there's some kind of official procedure to go through to cancel the book? But I never even signed the contract!"

"This isn't about the book, Nickie. It's about us. You didn't think I was just going to let you walk out of my life, did you, darling?"

Before she could question him further, his arms were around her, pressing her against his massive chest. "I could hold you this way forever," he murmured, his breath warm in her ear. "But you really have to change your clothes. The Weldons are very proper people."

"The Weldons!" She looked up into his face and tried to fathom the cryptic expression she saw there.

"They just returned from a cruise yesterday, or I would have been in touch sooner. I've told them everything—about Shields, the biography, you. Mostly about you, darling. That's why they insist on talking to you themselves."

"They're going to tell me . . . ?"

"I don't know, Nickie. They didn't tell me what they plan to say."

"Well, we'll just have to see then," she said softly. "I'll go change."

A few minutes later, she emerged from the bedroom wearing a light gray seersucker suit and darker gray pumps. Rob smiled his approval and put a proprietary arm around her waist as they left the loft together and descended to the street, where Burns was waiting for them with the limousine.

Nickie soon realized that the car was following the familiar route to Rob's penthouse on Park Avenue. Suddenly, it occurred to her that this might all be a trick, a ruse. "Rob, if you're planning to—to abduct me, take me to your apartment . . ." she faltered.

"Nickie, you gave me your ultimatum, now I'm giving you mine. For once in your life, you have to trust me."

Strangely, she did. And although the limousine did continue on to Rob's building, it didn't stop there but went further uptown, turning on Eighty-first Street to go down Fifth Avenue, where Burns eventually pulled up before a landmark brownstone.

"No telling how long we'll be, so you'd better not wait, Burns," Rob instructed the chauffeur. "I'll call you later if necessary."

A uniformed maid answered the doorbell and ushered them into a high-ceilinged living room where an aristocratic-looking couple were sitting together on a Louis XV couch in front of a marble fireplace. Nickie immediately saw the resemblance to Joan in Anne Weldon's high cheekbones and classic features, though the white-haired woman with sad eyes who stared at the carpet as her husband rose to greet them seemed old enough to be the dead woman's grandmother. Nickie knew instinctively that tragedy had aged Mrs. Weldon.

Mr. Weldon, too, looked haggard and mournful. Like his wife, he had snow-white hair, and frown lines were etched into his forehead. "Rob," he acknowledged the younger man in a deep voice as they shook hands. Then he turned to Nickie. "It was good of you to come to us, Miss Monroe. Won't you sit down?"

"Thank you," she murmured, letting Rob lead her to an armchair. He took the matching seat that faced it, across from the sofa where the Weldons sat.

Then, to Nickie's horror, she realized that Mrs. Weldon had begun to cry quietly. Tears bathed her pale cheeks. "I'm sorry," the older woman apologized as she continued to weep. "This has all been very hard."

Frank Weldon fumbled in his pocket for a handkerchief, but Rob had already produced one, which Mrs. Weldon accepted with visible gratitude.

"There, there, Anne," her husband comforted awkwardly. "You mustn't get upset. Your heart..."

Mrs. Weldon struggled to compose her features. "I'm all right now," she said with an embarrassed look at Nickie. "Forgive me, Miss Monroe. It's just that seeing Rob again brings back so many memories, and you're just about the age Joan would be."

Nickie was moved by the woman's grief. "Please," she said, "there's nothing to forgive. Rather, I feel I should beg your pardon for intruding on your sorrow."

"No, we asked you here," Mr. Weldon said. "It's not easy for us to talk about what happened. Joan was our only child. We've tried to protect her reputation and our own, but when Rob told us what's been going on, and we realized that our obstinacy was standing between him and the woman he loves..."

"It wasn't just obstinacy, Frank," Mrs. Weldon said. "We've been utterly selfish. Rob was so good to Joan. She used him, and we've used him, too. Instead of thinking how he would be affected, we've thought only of ourselves." She turned to Nickie with an expression of appeal. "What we're trying to say, Miss Monroe, is that you mustn't think Rob has been hiding anything shameful from you. It's our shame he's been covering, because we were selfish enough to ask it of him."

"Anne," Rob said gently, "I've never thought you were selfish. You've been through a lot, and it would be selfish of *me* to put you through another ordeal."

"You and Frank are afraid I'll have another heart attack, aren't you?" Mrs. Weldon said candidly. "But I'm stronger than you think. Breaking down the way I just did and crying seems to have done me a world of good. Perhaps if I allowed myself to let go a bit more often, I wouldn't have a heart condition. Miss Monroe," she went on, "Rob has told us about the biography. We want to know if you think that telling the true story about

Joan is really necessary to clear Rob's name."

"It's not," Rob answered swiftly. "If Nickie will stand by me, I don't give a rap what anyone else says."

Nickie met his gaze and said levelly, "I'll stand by you, Rob. But I think it's only fair to tell the Weldons that your name will be under a cloud if you let Shields's allegations stand unchallenged."

"Nickie—" Rob's voice was low, but held a warning note.

"She's quite right, Rob," Frank Weldon broke in quickly. "Thank you, Miss Monroe, for being honest."

"Yes, we want to do the right thing," Mrs. Weldon backed him up. "It will be better for us as well. At least for me, it's been the silence, even between ourselves, that's been so painful. Putting away all Joan's pictures, pretending she never existed . . . We're failing her again, just as we failed her when she was alive, when she was ill."

"Ill?" Nickie echoed, thinking that perhaps Mrs. Weldon's heart condition was hereditary. Although why there should be so much mystery about it, she couldn't fathom.

"Rob, why don't you tell her?" Frank Weldon suggested.

Rob nodded, and leaned forward in his chair. "Nickie," he said softly, "Joan had a venereal disease—someone she met in Rome—and it wasn't responding to penicillin or other drugs."

"You mean it was incurable?" Nickie said compassionately. "Poor Joan!"

"Yes, poor Joan," Mrs. Weldon repeated, her face crumpling. "You never knew our daughter, Miss Monroe, yet your reaction is to pity her. She had a right to expect that and more from her parents, but we . . ." Her voice trailed off, and she shook her head. "She was always so afraid of our disapproval. We were never demonstrative enough, never accepting enough. And when this came out, my first response was, 'How could you do this to us?' I hadn't a thought for her pain, her terror."

"It's the way Anne and I were brought up," Mr. Weldon explained. "It may be hard for you to understand, Miss Monroe. But the shock of it . . . Why, it had never occurred to us that she'd—she'd go with a man she wasn't married to. And this! We had no idea Joan even knew about such things. We'd done everything to shelter her, to protect her."

"We were *too* protective," Mrs. Weldon said. "That's why she wanted to stay in Rome—not to study art, but to find out about life, as she put it. If we hadn't brought Joan up so strictly, she'd be alive today. We'd have had grandchildren."

"Mrs. Weldon, I'm sure you and Mr. Weldon loved Joan very much," Nickie said consolingly. "Surely, she understood that you only did what you thought was best."

"We really did think our way was right," Mrs. Weldon said eagerly. "Thank you for understanding that, Miss Monroe. But we were wrong. We told ourselves we were giving Joan everything: the best education, a proper upbringing, a sense of values. What we actually gave her was our own morbid obsession with what people would think. She was hysterical when she finally brought herself to tell us about her . . . condition. She kept repeating, 'No one will ever know. Don't worry, I've got it all planned out. No one will ever know!'"

"She only told us because she thought we'd be better able to locate the right sort of doctor than she would," Mr. Weldon explained. "She'd been to various specialists in Europe without success. We did find someone here in New York, but he couldn't do anything except tell her there was sometimes a spontaneous remission in these sorts of cases."

"Rob, perhaps you should tell Miss Monroe where you fit into Joan's plan," Mrs. Weldon suggested. "I'm sure she must be wondering about that."

He cleared his throat reluctantly. "Joan had seen pictures of me with various socialites in the papers. She came to me with what she called a business proposition," he said.

"Our daughter had a large inheritance, her own money, from her grandparents," Mr. Weldon contributed. "She offered Rob a large sum of money to be her escort, to let other men think she was in love with him, so that she wouldn't have to cope with eligible men asking her out and that sort of thing. Actually, she seemed to want... well, almost a bodyguard. She was obsessed with the idea that someone would find out her secret. She knew I'd had some business dealings with Rob and thought highly of him, of his discretion. She thought the money would tempt him, what with his expanding business and all. But he never took a penny from Joan. He did everything she wanted out of sheer human sympathy. The sympathy we owed and didn't give her," he added, more to himself than to the others.

Rob gave a self-deprecating shrug. "I was on the rebound from a love affair of my own and had been feeling sorry for myself. When Joan came along with her story, I realized how self-indulgent I was being. I mean, here was someone who really had cause for unhappiness."

"He's being delicate," Mrs. Weldon told Nickie. "The fact is, Joan had become mentally unbalanced. Rob tried to give her some semblance of a normal life, keep her hopes up, make her feel less alone. We all tried to be optimistic about a remission. She was young and otherwise healthy, after all. But Joan was taking no chances. She had a kind of paranoia that people would find out, that she'd be mocked, sneered at. She had a secret plan. If the remission didn't occur within a certain period of time, she would commit suicide. Meanwhile, she was setting the stage for her obituary. Everyone was to think she had died of unrequited love. She wasn't really in

love with Rob—she was in no state to love anyone—
but she wanted to be remembered as some kind of romantic heroine. She left a note for the press, telling the
whole grandiose story she'd invented. We destroyed it,
never even told the police it existed. Because she'd gone
too far. She wanted Rob to marry her—someplace where
a blood test wouldn't be required, and yet she wanted
everyone to assume she'd had the test, so they wouldn't
guess . . ."

"We were grateful for all Rob had done for Joan. We
couldn't let that note become public," Mr. Weldon said.
"Yet we were all too eager to cover up the sordid facts,
and when people assumed that Joan *had* killed herself
out of unrequited love—well, we just let them assume
it."

"We knew nothing about her plan to kill herself until
we found the body," Mrs. Weldon said. "We always
refused to believe the disease would be terminal. We
prayed for her, and the doctor was encouraging. But
when the last round of test results turned out to be pos-
itive . . ."

"She was counting on us," Mr. Weldon said sadly.
"She knew we wouldn't want anyone to know, not only
about the disease, but also about the circumstances. You
see, in Rome, Joan had been rather . . . promiscuous. But
she had created a whole new image for herself in New
York, and she knew we'd do everything to maintain it.
The closed inquest, Rob's cooperation . . ."

"She had a right to do all she could to protect her
name and yours from the gossip hounds," Rob defended
the dead woman. "At heart, she blamed herself, and in
her own way was trying to make amends."

"But she's damaged you, Rob. I don't think she realized . . . or if she did, she didn't comprehend what this
would mean. It's our turn to make amends." Mrs. Weldon turned to Nickie, and for the first time, she smiled.

"You don't say much, Miss Monroe, but you have kind eyes. We would trust you to tell as much of all this as you think necessary and appropriate in your biography of Rob."

Nickie looked at Rob, love for him welling up in her heart, and shook her head. "No, Mrs. Weldon. I understand now why Rob never wanted that, and I think he's right. It would be as if he were trying to make himself look good, as if we were trying to capitalize on other people's unhappiness to sell the book. Thank you for your trust. It means a lot to me. But I don't think the biography is the place to—"

"But you have to finish your book," Mr. Weldon broke in. "And if you're silent about Joan, we'll be right back where we started, won't we? Unless . . ." He looked hesitantly at his wife. "Anne, maybe the best thing to do would be to tell it ourselves. We could write something up for *The New York Times*. We wouldn't even have to talk to a reporter. That way, Shields would have to retract his lies and there'd be no need at all for Rob to respond."

"That's a good idea, Frank. What do you think, Rob? Miss Monroe?"

"It's your decision," Rob said, and Nickie nodded. "Now I think we won't take up any more of your time . . ."

The Weldons rose with them, and everyone shook hands. Mrs. Weldon took Nickie to one side and said, "God bless you, my dear. Rob is a good man, and I hope you'll be very happy together."

"Thank you, Mrs. Weldon. I wish you and Mr. Weldon all the best, too."

Nickie and Rob walked in silence out to the street. Nickie felt as if a great burden had been lifted from her. Nothing remained between her and Rob to keep them apart. Her faith in him was confirmed; she was free to love him without restraint, free to trust him with all her heart.

But did he still love her? Did he still feel the same passion for her, the same need? Or had those emotions died forever when she'd walked out on him and forced him to choose between his love for her and his inviolate promise to the Weldons?

The warmth in his eyes when he'd appeared unexpectedly at her door had given her hope. Was she a fool to nurture that hope?

Finally Rob asked, "Are there any further questions you want to ask me, Nickie?"

She shook her head, made uneasy by his formal tone. "I think we can finally let Joan Weldon rest in peace. I only hope the Weldons can find some peace, too."

"So do I. Poor Joan was terrified of them. I guess that's what struck a chord in me. I was pretty terrified of my own father, always trying to win his approval."

She gazed up at him, her eyes wide with yearning. "Oh, Rob, if he were alive now, I'm certain he'd be as proud of you as I am," she assured him. Impulsively, she raised up on tiptoes and kissed his lips lingeringly.

Unmindful of the lunch-hour crowds of people hurrying past them, Rob gathered her into a fierce embrace. His lips were gentle and seductive, then urgent and demanding. He groaned softly and pulled away with a sigh. "Nickie, let's go." His large hand enveloped her smaller one. His long strides took them quickly down the few blocks to his apartment, Nickie almost running to keep up with him. Was she breathless from his kiss or from his rapid pace? All she knew was that a tentative joy was building up inside her; she felt giddy and light-headed, ready to burst.

Minutes later they reached his apartment door. He pushed it open impatiently, pulled her inside, and claimed her in a hungry embrace. His mouth was hot and probing. His hands sought to possess her.

At last they pulled apart, Nickie slightly dazed. She

could no longer doubt him, but her smile was wavery. Her question came shyly. "Does this mean you still want me?"

His laughter broke the final tension between them. His arms cradled her tenderly. "Yes, it means I still want you, you doubting Thomas," he assured her. "I want to make love to you, and I want to live with you, and I want to marry you." His expression turned serious, uncertain. "You will marry me, won't you?"

"Now who's full of doubt?" she teased fondly. "Yes, I'll make love to you." Her kiss hinted at just how steamy that lovemaking would be. "And, yes, I'll live with you—as long as I can set up my own office." She bit him playfully on the ear. "And, yes, I'll marry you—and live with you in wedded bliss for the rest of our lives."

"And you'll write your novel?"

"Right after I finish the biography of the great Thomas Robinson Starr."

"You're a very impartial biographer, aren't you?"

"Completely objective," she confirmed proudly.

"And is this completely objective writer ready to make up for lost time?"

"You mean the biography?" she asked mischievously, linking her arm through his.

He grinned. "You know what I mean. After lunch, remind me to give Burns the afternoon off."

Later, as they lay in Rob's enormous bed, caressing one another and exchanging endearments, he said, "You know, darling, you still have a secret from me."

"What do you mean?" she asked, puzzled, her hand lingering on his chest.

"You never did tell me what your novel is about. Is it autobiographical?"

The idea made her smile. "It's about a piano prodigy, actually. And if we ever get around to playing that piano duet, you'll see just how *un*autobiographical it is."

"Oh, I don't know about that," he said, nuzzling her ear. "There are prodigies and then there are prodigies. You're a prodigy here"—he kissed her lips—"and here"—his lips moved to one breast—"and here"—he kissed the other breast.

As she melted into the curve of his lean body, Nickie felt that, indeed, there could be nothing more prodigious, nothing more extraordinary and wonderful, than the perfect love between them. She knew it would last forever.

____ 07215-X **JADE TIDE #127** Jena Hunt $1.95
____ 07216-8 **THE MARRYING KIND #128** Jocelyn Day $1.95
____ 07217-6 **CONQUERING EMBRACE #129** Ariel Tierney $1.95
____ 07218-4 **ELUSIVE DAWN #130** Kay Robbins $1.95
____ 07219-2 **ON WINGS OF PASSION #131** Beth Brookes $1.95
____ 07220-6 **WITH NO REGRETS #132** Nuria Wood $1.95
____ 07221-4 **CHERISHED MOMENTS #133** Sarah Ashley $1.95
____ 07222-2 **PARISIAN NIGHTS #134** Susanna Collins $1.95
____ 07233-0 **GOLDEN ILLUSIONS #135** Sarah Crewe $1.95
____ 07224-9 **ENTWINED DESTINIES #136** Rachel Wayne $1.95
____ 07225-7 **TEMPTATION'S KISS #137** Sandra Brown $1.95
____ 07226-5 **SOUTHERN PLEASURES #138** Daisy Logan $1.95
____ 07227-3 **FORBIDDEN MELODY #139** Nicola Andrews $1.95
____ 07228-1 **INNOCENT SEDUCTION #140** Cally Hughes $1.95
____ 07229-X **SEASON OF DESIRE #141** Jan Mathews $1.95
____ 07230-3 **HEARTS DIVIDED #142** Francine Rivers $1.95
____ 07231-1 **A SPLENDID OBSESSION #143** Francesca Sinclaire $1.95
____ 07232-X **REACH FOR TOMORROW #144** Mary Haskell $1.95
____ 07233-8 **CLAIMED BY RAPTURE #145** Marie Charles $1.95
____ 07234-6 **A TASTE FOR LOVING #146** Frances Davies $1.95
____ 07235-4 **PROUD POSSESSION #147** Jena Hunt $1.95
____ 07236-2 **SILKEN TREMORS #148** Sybil LeGrand $1.95
____ 07237-0 **A DARING PROPOSITION #149** Jeanne Grant $1.95
____ 07238-9 **ISLAND FIRES #150** Jocelyn Day $1.95
____ 07239-7 **MOONLIGHT ON THE BAY #151** Maggie Peck $1.95
____ 07240-0 **ONCE MORE WITH FEELING #152** Melinda Harris $1.95
____ 07241-9 **INTIMATE SCOUNDRELS #153** Cathy Thacker $1.95
____ 07242-7 **STRANGER IN PARADISE #154** Laurel Blake $1.95
____ 07243-5 **KISSED BY MAGIC #155** Kay Robbins $1.95
____ 07244-3 **LOVESTRUCK #156** Margot Leslie $1.95
____ 07245-1 **DEEP IN THE HEART #157** Lynn Lawrence $1.95
____ 07246-X **SEASON OF MARRIAGE #158** Diane Crawford $1.95
____ 07247-8 **THE LOVING TOUCH #159** Aimée Duvall $1.95
____ 07575-2 **TENDER TRAP #160** Charlotte Hines $1.95
____ 07576-0 **EARTHLY SPLENDOR #161** Sharon Francis $1.95
____ 07577-9 **MIDSUMMER MAGIC #162** Kate Nevins $1.95
____ 07578-7 **SWEET BLISS #163** Daisy Logan $1.95
____ 07579-5 **TEMPEST IN EDEN #164** Sandra Brown $1.95
____ 07580-9 **STARRY EYED #165** Maureen Norris #1.95

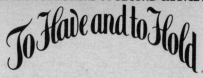

WHAT READERS SAY ABOUT
SECOND CHANCE AT LOVE BOOKS

"I can't begin to thank you for the many, many hours of pure bliss I have received from the wonderful SECOND CHANCE [AT LOVE] books. Everyone I talk to lately has admitted their preference for SECOND CHANCE [AT LOVE] over all the other lines."
    —*S. S., Phoenix, AZ**

"Hurrah for Berkley . . . the butterfly and its wonderful SECOND CHANCE AT LOVE."
    —*G. B., Mount Prospect, IL**

"Thank you, thank you, thank you—I just had to write to let you know how much I love SECOND CHANCE AT LOVE . . . "
    —*R. T., Abbeville, LA**

"It's so hard to wait 'til it's time for the next shipment . . . I hope your firm soon considers adding to the line."
    —*P. D., Easton, PA**

"SECOND CHANCE AT LOVE is fantastic. I have been reading romances for as long as I can remember—and I enjoy SECOND CHANCE [AT LOVE] the best."
    —*G. M., Quincy, IL**

*Names and addresses available upon request